MOON OVER EDEN

Barbara Cartland

Barbara Cartland Ebooks Ltd

This edition © 2018

Copyright Cartland Promotions 1976

ISBNs

9781788670692   EPUB
9781788670708   PAPERBACK

Book design by M-Y Books
m-ybooks.co.uk

THE BARBARA CARTLAND ETERNAL COLLECTION

The Barbara Cartland Eternal Collection is the unique opportunity to collect all five hundred of the timeless beautiful romantic novels written by the world's most celebrated and enduring romantic author.

Named the Eternal Collection because Barbara's inspiring stories of pure love, just the same as love itself, the books will be published on the internet at the rate of four titles per month until all five hundred are available.

The Eternal Collection, classic pure romance available worldwide for all time .

THE LATE DAME BARBARA CARTLAND

Barbara Cartland, who sadly died in May 2000 at the grand age of ninety eight, remains one of the world's most famous romantic novelists. With worldwide sales of over one billion, her outstanding 723 books have been translated into thirty six different languages, to be enjoyed by readers of romance globally.

Writing her first book 'Jigsaw' at the age of 21, Barbara became an immediate bestseller. Building upon this initial success, she wrote continuously throughout her life, producing bestsellers for an astonishing 76 years. In addition to Barbara Cartland's legion of fans in the UK and across Europe, her books have always been immensely popular in the USA. In 1976 she achieved the unprecedented feat of having books at numbers 1 & 2 in the prestigious B. Dalton Bookseller bestsellers list.

Although she is often referred to as the 'Queen of Romance', Barbara Cartland also wrote several historical biographies, six autobiographies and numerous theatrical plays as well as books on life, love, health and cookery. Becoming one of Britain's most popular media personalities and dressed in her trademark pink, Barbara spoke on radio and television about social and political issues, as well as making many public appearances.

In 1991 she became a Dame of the Order of the British Empire for her contribution to literature and her work for humanitarian and charitable causes.

Known for her glamour, style, and vitality Barbara Cartland became a legend in her own lifetime. Best remembered for her wonderful romantic novels and loved by millions of readers worldwide, her books remain treasured for their heroic heroes, plucky heroines and traditional values. But above all, it was Barbara Cartland's overriding belief in the positive power of love to help, heal and improve the quality of life for everyone that made her truly unique.

AUTHOR'S NOTE

I visited Sri Lanka in 1975 and was thrilled with the exquisite almost unbelievable beauty of the country, the charm and friendliness of its people and I was fascinated by its history.

The background of this book is all authentic and the success of Ceylon tea after the failure of coffee was immortalised by Sir Arthur Conan Doyle when he wrote,

"Not often is it that men have the heart, when their one great industry is withered, to rear up in a few years another as rich to take its place and the tea fields of Ceylon are as true a monument to courage as is the lion at Waterloo."

James Taylor was not only the first man on the island to grow tea commercially but he also manufactured and sold it. His enterprise as an attempt to retrieve the tragedy of coffee, which ruined thousands of people, became a sparkle of hope in Ceylon's economy. When he died his labourers called him *Sami Durai*, 'the Master who is God'.

In 1873 the export of tea from Sri Lanka was just twenty-eight pounds in weight and one hundred years later it was more than four hundred and forty-five million pounds in weight.

CHAPTER ONE
1888

Lord Hawkston drew in a deep breath of the warm moist air.

He looked up at the starlit sky and knew how much he had missed in the cold of England and this warmth that seemed to percolate his whole body, made him feel as if every muscle had become loose and supple.

He walked slowly across the grass, conscious of the fragrance of the magnolias, the lovely moonflower of the jasmines and the oleanders, their branches in the daytime providing a welcome shelter from the heat of the sun.

During the twenty-six days of the voyage from England he had looked forward to seeing Ceylon again almost like a small boy going home for the holidays.

It was not surprising, seeing that he had spent sixteen years of his life in what was called an 'Island Paradise' where, according to the Mohammedans, Adam and Eve had sought refuge after they were driven away from the Garden of Eden.

In England it had been easy to laugh at such descriptions as that of the Brahmins, 'Lanka, the resplendent' or the Buddhists, 'the pearl drop on the brow of India' or the Greeks, 'the land of lotus flowers'.

But back in Ceylon the mystique of the climate and the beauty of the country made Lord Hawkston feel that they did not exaggerate.

Not that he was a romantic person. He was known for being ultra-reserved, a hard taskmaster and ruthless when it suited him.

He had had to be because his life had not been easy. In fact he had succeeded only by fighting every inch of the way for what he wanted and by being absolutely certain of what he did want.

As he strolled further into the magnificent garden of the Queen's House, as the Governor-General's residence in Colombo was known, he thought that, when he went North to his tea plantation, it would be like a Royal progress to see his friends again, his coolies and the fine house he had built himself on the site of the small cottage that had originally been his home when he had first bought the plantation.

Deep in his thoughts it was with a sense of irritation that Lord Hawkston suddenly realised that he was no longer alone in the garden.

He had waited until the Governor and his other guests had retired to their rooms before he walked out into the moonlit night, having an irresistible urge to be alone with his memories and his emotions at coming back.

Now someone else was coming across the lawn.

Instinctively, because he had no wish for conversation, Lord Hawkston stood still in the shadow of a large bamboo knowing that he was half-concealed by its feathery branches and that unless someone was deliberately seeking him out he was unlikely to be aware of his presence.

The man came nearer and now because the moonlight was full on his face Lord Hawkston was aware that it was a young soldier who had travelled out to Ceylon with him on the same ship.

Captain Patrick O'Neill had been one of several Officers returning from furlough to their military duties.

Lord Hawkston had conversed with them at meals because they were seated, as he was, at the Captain's table, but otherwise he had associated as little as possible with the younger passengers who, he felt, would think him too old to take part in their spirited chatter and incessant teasing of one another.

At the same time Patrick O'Neill, Lord Hawkston remembered, had seemed a trifle more responsible than the rest and he imagined that he would become an able Officer in his Regiment.

Still the Captain advanced and Lord Hawkston, waiting in the shadows, thought that perhaps he was in charge of the sentries guarding the Governor and was intent at this hour of the night on seeing that they were doing their duty.

Then to his surprise, just before he reached the tree where Lord Hawkston was concealed, Captain O'Neill turned and walked across the grass directly towards the house.

Like most Colonial houses the Queen's House was extremely impressive in the front but the back rambled away into long verandahs on two floors where, in the heat of the summer months, the inhabitants slept, but which in February were unscreened and open to the night air.

It was with a sense of relief that Lord Hawkston realised that he was not in danger of being discovered.

Then, as he watched Captain O'Neill reach the back of the house, he saw him look up at the verandah above him and heard him give a soft low whistle.

Surprised, Lord Hawkston waited and saw someone in white come from the bedroom and on to the verandah where Captain O'Neill was standing.

It was a woman! Her hair was loose and it fell forward in a fair cloud as she reached the rail of the verandah and bent over it.

If she spoke Lord Hawkston could not hear what she said, but to his astonishment. Captain O'Neill, who had been standing looking up at her, started to climb up from the ground to the verandah above him.

It was not a difficult task for the supporting pillars were made of open wrought-ironwork, affording an excellent foothold for even the clumsiest of mountaineers.

It was only a matter of seconds before the Captain flung his leg over the railing and stepped on to the verandah.

Then, as Lord Hawkston watched, he saw him take the woman in his arms and they clung together in a passionate embrace.

For a moment they stood in the moonlight, embodying the eternal figure of love, their arms around each other, their lips joined and the woman's hair pale against the Captain's broad shoulder.

Then they moved away and disappeared into the darkness of the bedroom behind them.

Lord Hawkston drew in his breath.

He was well aware who it was Captain O'Neill was visiting in this clandestine way and for a moment he felt not anger but sheer astonishment at the audacity of it.

For the woman whom Captain O'Neill had kissed so passionately and with whom he had vanished was the Honourable Emily Ludgrove, whom Lord Hawkston had brought out with him to Ceylon to marry his nephew, Gerald Warren!

*

When, eighteen years earlier, Lord Hawkston, then Chilton Hawk, had decided to go to Ceylon he had been twenty-one and the younger son of a younger son.

There had been no prospect of his ever inheriting the family title and estates and his father, who had very little money, could offer no inducements for a comfortable life in England.

He had, however, inherited two thousand pounds when he attained his majority and, inspired by a report he had read of the success of the coffee plantations in Ceylon, he decided to visit the country and try to make his fortune.

Ceylon in those days seemed very far away and people spoke of it in England as if it was the other end of the world.

Ten years earlier in 1860 there had been a boom in coffee after the British planters had brought with them a spirit of enterprise as well as capital to invest in the plantations.

Chilton Hawk had been at Oxford with a Scot who had gone to Ceylon three years earlier and wrote him enthusiastic letters of the opportunities that existed there for young men with energy and ambition.

On making enquiries Chilton Hawk found that in 1870, the year he came of age, Ceylon had shipped over one million hundredweight of coffee.

His father was surprised at his decision to be a coffee planter, although he had expected him to travel on the legacy he had inherited from his grandmother.

"Don't commit yourself, my boy," he had said. "Have a good look round first. You might do better in Singapore or India."

But the moment Chilton Hawk had reached Ceylon he realised this was where he wished to live and work.

And work he did!

He had not realised how hard it would be until he had bought five hundred and sixty acres of land at one pound an acre and found that he had to clear away the jungle from it.

This meant he had to employ eighty men and always there was the fear at the back of his mind that his money would run out.

He started the day with the click-clack of axes, the crash of falling trees and the noise of saws and hammers. Then everything had to be carted away and burnt.

It was not a question of merely felling the trees but of digging out every root before the land was ready for planting.

He had the luck almost as soon as he arrived of being introduced by his Oxford friend to an experienced thirty-five year old Scottish planter named James Taylor.

He was one of the planters who was to be part of the history of Ceylon and already he had an importance that made him respected by other planters.

At the age of eighteen, James Taylor, a vigorous young giant of a man, had signed a three year contract with the London agents of the Loolecondera Estate, which was situated some seventy miles South-East of Kandy.

The advantage of being near Kandy was that the railway to Colombo had been completed in 1867.

It afforded the planters a much more rapid form of transportation for their coffee than they could obtain with the plodding bullock carts, which took weeks to move slowly down the military road to the Port.

James Taylor took a fancy to the young man who had just come out from England and advised him to buy land near the Loolecondera Estate, which was in the central mountain region.

Like Taylor, Chilton Hawk had been enchanted by the scenic beauty of the hill country, and he soon adapted himself to his new strange environment.

James Taylor showed him how to obtain a labour force of Tamil coolies and advised him where to build his first small cottage.

He encouraged him and helped him through the first years of clearing and planting when Chilton Hawk worked as hard, if not harder, than any of the men he employed.

Yet, looking back, he had often thought that this was the happiest time in his life. He was achieving something. He was his own Master and, if he lost everything he possessed, he had no one to blame but himself.

And he would have lost everything if he had not been a friend of James Taylor.

For ten years the coffee boom had made Chilton Hawk believe that he was on the verge of becoming rich. Land rose to twenty-eight pounds an acre and cultivations extended along new roads that had been only the pilgrim paths to Adam's Peak.

Suddenly the halcyon days of coffee were numbered.

A dreaded leaf disease peculiar to coffee, known as *Hemileia Vastatrix* or 'coffee rust' threatened the whole industry.

Even now Lord Hawkston could remember the feeling of sick horror that he had felt when he first saw the fungus on his own coffee plants.

The fungus was a microscopic one and its spore was carried by the wind to settle and germinate on the leaves of the plants.

It was totally catastrophic for every coffee planter. There was nothing they could do except clear an infected plantation, powder the remaining trees with a mixture of lime and sulphur and pray they would not be re-infected when the next batch of spore was brought in on the wind.

It was a hope that did not materialise.

The coffee disease wrecked the aspirations of most European planters and all the Ceylonese.

There was nothing they could salvage from their ruined plantations except that some diseased coffee stumps were shipped to England to serve as legs for tea tables.

But for Chilton Hawk his friendship with James Taylor proved a lifeline.

Taylor had in 1866 been given some tea seedlings by the Superintendent of the Royal Botanical Gardens at Peradeniya,

Nineteen acres at Loolecondera were planted with two hundred pounds of tea seedlings and James Taylor, when he helped Chilton Hawk with his neighbouring land, persuaded him to plant the same number of acres of his precious soil with tea.

Those nineteen acres saved the estate from utter ruin.

It meant that on the rest of the plantation Chilton Hawk had to start again from scratch.

He rolled up his sleeves and planted tea.

Meanwhile his friend, Taylor, was busy on a new project, a fully equipped teahouse fitted with a rolling-machine, the first ever made in Ceylon.

Following the financial instability caused by the catastrophic crash of coffee, hopes rose when it became known that on Taylor's estate and the one adjoining his, tea was proving profitable.

Disillusioned coffee-planters went along to learn how to cultivate the new crop and all over Ceylon tea bushes began to thrive between the stumps of dead coffee trees.

Chilton Hawk, working twenty-four hours a day, began to build up once again the fortune he had lost.

He had never in his wildest moments thought that there was any chance of his inheriting the family estates in England.

There were six lives between him and the chance of being his uncle's heir when he had left England, but through death in battle, accident and the inescapability of old age, gradually those who preceded him were eliminated one by one.

Nevertheless in 1886 it came as an incredible shock to learn that his uncle was dead and that he was the new Lord Hawkston.

There was nothing he could do but go home, but it had been like amputating an arm or a leg to leave behind him his plantation, which had now expanded to one thousand two hundred acres, and his friends like James Taylor.

At the same time he had grown very self-sufficient. He had to be!

Sometimes three or four weeks would pass without his seeing anybody except for his coolies.

He would sit alone in the big house he had now built for himself on the top of a hill so that it caught all the breezes during the hot weather.

It could also be cold in winter and in English fashion it had large open fireplaces where logs could be burnt.

Chilton Hawk grew used to being by himself. He liked reading but more often than not, after he had enjoyed a well-cooked and well-served meal, he went to bed, so as to rise with the dawn and return to the work that absorbed him.

He had forgotten when he returned to England what an elegant leisurely life a gentleman could live without pressures, without haste and without any ambition except to fill the leisure hours with enjoyment.

He had, however, found a great deal to do on the family estate.

His uncle had been ill for the last years of his life and many things had been neglected. There were new farming methods to be introduced, machinery to be bought, buildings to be repaired and above all relations to meet.

While in Ceylon, Chilton Hawk had been a leader and organiser of a labour force, but in England as Lord Hawkston he was now expected to be the Head of a large Family of relations, most of them impecunious and all of them, he reflected dryly, grasping and avaricious.

His first task on returning home was to find someone who could take his place on the plantation in Ceylon.

This, he determined, would be a family possession in the future and be looked on as part of the inheritance of future owners of the title.

He thought that he had found the ideal person in his nephew, Gerald Warren, the only son of his elder sister, an intelligent young man of twenty-four.

Because he was so worried about the plantation being left with only his Ceylonese Head man in charge, Lord Hawkston had sent Gerald Warren out in a precipitate manner that he would not have considered had the matter not been so urgent.

He felt that Gerald, at twenty-four, should be quite capable of coping with an estate that was running smoothly and making a profit and where there was no longer the heavy manual fundamental work to do that had been his task sixteen years earlier.

Gerald had been only too willing to acquiesce to everything his uncle suggested.

Lord Hawkston was to learn later that he was not particularly happy at home and had in fact fallen out with most of his other relatives.

He had, however, just before he sailed, declared himself engaged to the daughter of a neighbouring Nobleman, the Honourable Emily Ludgrove, but her family had dissuaded them from getting married before Gerald left.

They had for some time discouraged any talk of a betrothal for the simple reason that Gerald had few prospects and showed no inclination to obtain any more money than the small allowance that his widowed mother was prepared to give him.

His uncle's interest in him opened up new vistas and, although the engagement was not announced, it was agreed that Gerald and Emily should marry in a year's time.

"I will bring her out to Ceylon myself," Lord Hawkston had promised.

"Must we wait a year for you to do so?" Gerald asked.

"I am afraid so," his uncle replied. "There is so much for me to do here that I think it unlikely I will get away in under twelve months."

As a matter of fact it was eighteen months before there was a chance of his leaving England and Emily seemed quite content to wait until an opportune moment presented itself.

Her family was adamant that there was no need for a hurried marriage and, even after Lord Hawkston was ready to leave, small details of Emily's trousseau held them up for a further two months.

Finally they set sail from Southampton and Lord Hawkston cabled his nephew to meet them in Colombo.

He had noticed that Gerald's letters had been falling off during the past nine months.

At first he had written regularly and every fortnight a letter would arrive full of details about the plantation.

It was only lately that Lord Hawkston had begun to wonder if Gerald wrote what he thought his uncle would like to hear rather than what was actually occurring.

Then his letters arrived once a month and finally had tailed off into quick scribbles at intervals of two or even three months.

'The boy is busy,' Lord Hawkston told himself. 'I expect Emily hears from him regularly.'

He saw very little of Gerald's future wife. He found her father an extremely dull man who he had little in common with and in any case there was too much for him to do on the estate for him to have much time for social engagements.

In any case he found them irksome.

He had grown so used to being alone that social chitchat and petty gossip bored him.

He was well aware that his relations not only found him difficult but were in awe of him. He did not mind that being their attitude and on the whole he preferred it.

"He is a difficult man," he had heard one of his cousins say just as he was entering the drawing room. "I never have any idea what he is thinking and quite frankly I am not really interested to find out."

There had been the sound of laughter as the lady finished speaking but Lord Hawkston, waiting to make his entrance, had merely been amused.

On the ship he had gone out of his way to be as uncommunicative as possible.

He knew only too well that the gushing friendships of shipboard acquaintances seldom lasted once the passengers had reached dry land.

He was aware that Emily, who was chaperoned by a Colonel and his wife returning to duty in Colombo, was receiving plenty of attention from the young Army Officers on board.

She was obviously amused by the dancing and charades, the fancy dress parties and the ship's concerts that were arranged in the evenings.

He had not noticed, Lord Hawkston thought, that Captain Patrick O'Neill was more attentive to Emily than anyone else.

Now, standing in the garden of Queen's House, he blamed himself for not being more perceptive, for not having realised that the girl had lost her heart and certainly her head on the journey to Ceylon,

Lord Hawkston came from the shadow of the bamboo and walked across the lawn.

This was a situation he had not anticipated and he wondered what the devil he should do about it.

Of one thing he was certain. He had no intention of allowing Emily to marry his nephew.

Perhaps, he told himself, it was a good thing that Gerald had not been able to meet them in Colombo as he had expected.

The letter that had been waiting for him at Queen's House when they arrived told him that Gerald was too ill to travel, but hoped to be well enough to receive his uncle and Emily when they arrived in Kandy.

When he had first read the letter, Lord Hawkston had been annoyed.

He had already planned that Emily and Gerald should be married in Colombo immediately on his arrival.

He had thought that he would send them off on honeymoon and go up to the plantation alone.

He had looked forward to seeing what had been done, to discussing innovations with his Head man and greeting the coolies, some of whom had been with him since the very first day he had started to clear the jungle.

But his arrangements had been upset and he supposed that the Ceremony would have to take place in Kandy.

At this moment it was almost like a blow to realise that there would now be no Wedding and he would have to break the news to Gerald that he must look elsewhere for a wife.

'Damn the girl!' Lord Hawkston said to himself. 'Why the hell could she not behave herself?'

Even as he swore he realised that he himself was in part to blame for not having gone out to Ceylon sooner.

Eighteen months was a long time in two young people's lives. And years ago it had seemed a long time to him.

Equally if Emily was flighty enough to be beguiled away from Gerald by the first handsome young man who sought her favours, it was better for it to happen before marriage than after.

'I will send her home on the next ship,' Lord Hawkston decided.

The beauty of the night was spoilt for him and he turned and walked back to the front of the house, trying not to think of those two young people clasped in each other's arms in an upstairs bedroom.

*

The next morning Lord Hawkston breakfasted early. As he finished and was about to rise from the table he was told that there was someone to see him.

Surprised at so early a visitor he followed the servant, resplendent in his red and white uniform, down the wide corridors to a sitting room where to his delight he found James Taylor waiting for him.

At fifty Taylor was a very big man with a long beard. He weighed two hundred and fifty pounds and one of his fingers was as thick as three of an ordinary man's fingers put together.

When he smiled, it gave his face with its deep-set eyes and long nose a strange charm.

"I heard that you arrived yesterday, Chilton," he said, holding out his hand.

"James! By all that's Holy! I was hoping to see you but not so soon. How are you? It seems a century since we last met."

"I have missed you, Chilton," James Taylor said. "I began to be afraid that you had become too grand to come back to us."

"If only you knew how much I have longed to return before now!" Lord Hawkston replied. "But I have been working almost as hard at home as I did here, only in a different way. It has not been easy."

James Taylor smiled.

"Nothing you and I have done has ever been easy, Chilton, but I expect you have managed to win through."

"I hope so," Lord Hawkston answered.

Then he thought of Emily and his expression darkened.

"Tell me about my nephew."

"That is one of the reasons why I came here to see you."

There was something in the way he spoke that made Lord Hawkston look at him sharply.

"Has the boy settled down and done a good job?" he asked. "I want the truth."

"The whole truth?" James Taylor enquired.

"You know I would not be satisfied with anything less."

"Very well. We are old friends, Chilton, and because you and I have always been frank with each other I had to come to tell you that you will have to do something about that young man."

"What do you mean?" Lord Hawkston asked.

James Taylor hesitated for a moment before he said,

"I think, unlike you and me, he cannot adjust himself to the solitude. It is hard, as we both know, to live alone, to face long evenings with no one to talk to and to realise that one has to ride perhaps miles to find a friendly face."

James Taylor spoke quietly and there was a note of sympathy in his voice, but Lord Hawkston's tone was hard as he enquired,

"What is he doing – drinking?"

James Taylor nodded.

"What else?"

"He is messing things up rather badly."

"In what way?"

For a moment there was no answer and Lord Hawkston said,

"Tell me the truth, James, and I don't want it tied up with blue ribbon."

"Very well then," James Taylor said. "Speaking frankly he has broken the rules where a native girl is concerned."

Lord Hawkston stiffened.

"How can he have done that?"

"We both know," James Taylor' replied, "that it is quite usual and in no way reprehensible for a young man to take a mistress from a nearby village or another plantation."

Lord Hawkston nodded.

What was forbidden was for a planter to approach or be involved with one of his own employees.

"Your nephew made a Ceylonese girl his mistress a month after he arrived. Now he has kicked her out and refused to pay."

Lord Hawkston rose to his feet.

"I can hardly believe that!"

"It is true nevertheless and, as you can imagine, it has caused quite an upset."

Lord Hawkston was silent for a moment and then he said,

"Tell me every detail. I want to know."

He was well aware as he spoke that the rules of co-habitation between white men who were owners or managers of plantations with a native girl was an age-old custom and as such accepted by both the planters and the natives themselves.

The Portuguese and Dutch who preceded the English in Ceylon had taken women to live with them and in many cases married them.

The English had quite a different arrangement.

A planter living alone would take a mistress on the terms usually arranged by her father. He would invite her to his house when he needed her but she lived in a nearby village or even on the compound but not openly with him.

The girls were highly attractive, gentle and loving and a young planter could often find real happiness with one of them.

It was considered by the Ceylonese an honour that one of their women should be the mistress of the *Durai* or Master of a plantation and if a man tired of a woman there was no stigma attached to her.

She went back to her own people with a dowry that ensured she could marry one of her own kind, because in their eyes she was rich.

The number of rupees that should be given in compensation was more or less an unwritten law and accepted by both parties.

If there were children from the association, they lived with their mother and many of them moved to a certain village in the hills, which was known among the natives as 'New England'.

These children were surprisingly beautiful with dark skins and blue eyes and sometimes even fair hair.

They could, of course, cause trouble in that the parents of the girl realised that a child was an excuse to extort money from the father.

The reckoning was always high, sometimes crippling. An astute peasant would have a settlement drawn up by a properly qualified Proctor, a Solicitor, in the bazaar and an unfortunate young planter could find that he was saddled with a form of alimony for the rest of his life in Ceylon.

But in the majority of cases such unions were pleasant and, as long as justice was done, were without repercussions.

That Gerald should have been so stupid and obtuse as to have broken the rules that governed such arrangements was almost beyond Lord Hawkston's comprehension.

The planters in Ceylon were noted as being among the most intelligent, gentlemanly and trustworthy of any colonists in British dependences.

A microcosm of the population of Great Britain, elementary, grammar and public school boys. University graduates, businessmen, Lawyers, Officers of the Armed Services, Conservatives, Liberals, English, Scots, Welsh and Irish was the wide ranging spectrum to be found on the coffee, tea and rubber estates.

They worked hard, but they also played hard and once acclimatised enjoyed life immensely.

Few had had to pioneer their way as James Taylor and Chilton Hawk had been forced to do.

But it was still a rough life and to rise from a novice or 'creeper' to a *Perya Durai* or Big Master, as the coolies called them, entailed working from six o'clock in the morning to six or seven in the evening.

But a *Perya Durai* lived in a spacious bungalow or house set on a hilltop with large gardens. He did his round of the 'field' on horseback.

When he had leave, he could shoot wild elephants, elk, buffalo, bear and leopards, fish, swim, play cricket, hunt, take part in gymkhanas or polo tournaments and join the British Clubs that were within a day's journey of most plantations.

James Taylor explained very carefully what had happened.

Gerald had been drinking ever since he arrived. He had soon become bored with the plantation and everything had been left to the Head man.

Gerald had at first gone down to Kandy where there was a certain amount of amusement to be found, then he had joined the less reputable planters who enjoyed themselves in Colombo and paid little or no attention to their plantations.

This had kept him occupied for some time, but soon he found that his money was running out and he could not afford the visits, which always proved expensive.

Finally, because he was hard-up, Gerald was forced to sit in his house and drink, his only amusement being Seetha, the native girl who had taken his fancy soon after he arrived.

"What happened then?" Lord Hawkston asked.

"I gather that there was a scene a month ago, when Gerald had been drinking very heavily," James Taylor answered. "He accused the girl of stealing a signet ring that he always wore. Afterwards, I believe, it was discovered under a piece of furniture in the room."

He paused and his voice was scathing as he went on,

"At the time he was quite adamant that Seetha had stolen it and she was extremely angry and distressed knowing that she had done nothing of the sort."

Lord Hawkston could imagine how indignant the girl would be. The Ceylonese employed on the plantation were usually scrupulously honest and anyway were far too frightened to take anything that did not belong to them from their Master's house.

He himself had never missed anything all the years that he had lived in the hills.

"Gerald told the girl to clear out," James Taylor continued, "and, because he alleged that she was a thief, he refused to give her the money as is usual upon dismissal."

Lord Hawkston rose to walk across the room.

"The fool!" he exclaimed. "The damned fool."

"I agree with you," James Taylor said. "When I heard what had happened, I rode over to see the boy, but he was at that moment quite incapable of understanding anything I had to say. However I saw your cable to him lying on his desk. I read it, learnt that you were arriving and came here to tell you what was happening."

"That was kind of you, James."

"In the cable," James Taylor went on, "you put '*Emily and I arriving on Friday*'. Does it mean that you have brought Gerald a wife? I heard rumours that you were to do so. As you know, everything is known in such a small community."

"I brought with me a young woman who was engaged to Gerald before he left England," Lord Hawkston replied in a hard voice. "Unfortunately, I have discovered that her interests lie elsewhere and I shall not permit the marriage."

James Taylor gave a low whistle.

"More problems. Well, I must say, Chilton, I think it's a pity. I am sure if there is one thing that could save young Gerald it would be for him to have a sensible wife who would stop him drinking and disperse the loneliness and isolation that he obviously cannot endure alone."

"I will try to find him a wife," Lord Hawkston said, but he added beneath his breath, "it will *not* be Emily Ludgrove."

James Taylor looked at his watch.

"I must get back. I intend to catch the morning train to Kandy, but I wanted to prepare you for what lay ahead.

I hope you will be able to sort everything out, Chilton, and then come and see me. I have some interesting new experiments to show you."

"You know perfectly well that there is nothing I would enjoy more," Lord Hawkston replied. "Thank you, James, for proving yourself a true friend once again."

"I wish I had better news to bring you," James Taylor remarked. "But I will tell you one thing that will please you, the export of tea will reach over five million hundredweight this year."

Lord Hawkston smiled.

"That is the sort of information I certainly hoped to hear."

"My plantation is booming," James Taylor said, "and yours should do so if once again it has your magic touch. We need you back, Chilton. We all need you and so does Ceylon."

"Don't tempt me!" Lord Hawkston smiled. "You know I would rather be here than anywhere else in the world."

There was a ring of truth in his voice that was unmistakable and James Taylor put his hand on his friend's shoulder.

"I will be seeing you later, Chilton," he said. "We will talk about it then."

Lord Hawkston saw him to the door and then turned back with a frown between his eyes.

He knew now that he had to see Emily Ludgrove.

Then he had to decide what he would say to his nephew.

It was not a pleasant prospect and yet those who knew him well, had they seen the sudden tightening of his jaw, would have been aware that Chilton Hawk was about to go into battle and, as always, emerge victorious.

Twenty minutes later Emily Ludgrove came into the sitting room where Lord Hawkston waited for her. She was looking, he had to admit, extremely pretty.

The gown she had bought in London was in the very latest fashion and revealed the perfection of her slim figure, while the colour accentuated the blue of her eyes and the almost dazzling gold of her hair.

For almost the first time Lord Hawkston realised that she was indeed lovely and he thought perhaps it had been an absurd idea that she should incarcerate herself on a tea plantation miles away from the many admirers her beauty would attract.

"Good morning, my Lord," Emily said in a coquettish way with the look in her eyes that she accorded any man, young or old, when she was alone with him.

"Good morning, Emily," Lord Hawkston replied. "Will you please sit down? I wish to talk to you."

"That sounds ominous!" Emily exclaimed. "Is anything wrong?"

"I wish to inform you," Lord Hawkston said, "that I am arranging for your passage back to England on the first available ship."

He saw Emily's eyes widen in an incredulous look of surprise and went on before she could speak,

"I happened to be in the garden last night when Captain O'Neill visited you in a somewhat irregular manner."

For a moment Emily was still and then she said,

"Captain O'Neill has asked me to marry him."

"I should imagine that is the least he could do," Lord Hawkston remarked dryly.

"And I was just debating," Emily Ludgrove went on, "as to whether I should accept his offer."

"The choice is quite simple," Lord Hawkston said. "Either you accept Captain O'Neill or I send you back to England."

"Then I think you know, my Lord, "what my answer will be," Emily Ludgrove said with a smile. "You will, I am sure, make my apologies to Gerald, but I doubt if we should have found much happiness together after being apart for so long."

She rose from the sofa as she spoke and Lord Hawkston could not help thinking that she had accepted the situation with a poise that he would not have expected of her.

"If you have nothing more to say to me, my Lord," she went on, "I will retire and write a letter to Captain O'Neill, making him, he assures me, the happiest man in the world."

"I have nothing more to say," Lord Hawkston said. "I feel that you would not be interested in hearing my opinion of your behaviour."

"Why should I be?" Emily replied. "You don't understand, or else you have forgotten, what it is like to be young! One is old a long time, so I intend to enjoy myself while I can and there are men who are only too anxious to help me."

There was nothing that Lord Hawkston felt he could answer to this and he bowed rather ironically as Emily swept away from him towards the door.

She turned back as she reached it.

"Please tell Gerald," she said in dulcet tones, "how very much I regret making him miserable and say that I hope we shall always be friends."

She went from the room before Lord Hawkston could think of a suitable retort. Then despite his anger at her behaviour he could not help laughing.

She certainly had a nerve that he would not have anticipated and he felt that if anyone might have kept Gerald in order it would have been Emily Ludgrove.

At the same time he was quite sure that she was right. She would never have stood the loneliness of a plantation in the hill country and even if they had come to Colombo or returned to England he was certain that Emily would not have been content with Gerald.

Somehow she would have contrived that a number of other men were available to lay their hearts at her feet and, if meanwhile she hurt her husband's feelings, it would be something that he would have to put up with.

Lord Hawkston sighed.

That was one chapter closed.

Now there was Gerald to contend with and he was quite certain that James Taylor was right when he had said that what the boy needed was a sensible wife.

The trouble was where to find one?

He stood looking out at the garden. The flowers were a blaze of colour, there were purple orchids, the crimson hibiscus, and the white trumpet-like flowers of the frangipani or Temple trees.

It looked a perfect setting for love, but Lord Hawkston told himself that he was the last person capable of choosing a wife for his nephew.

After all he had been unable to choose one for himself and at thirty-seven he had come to the conclusion that he would remain a bachelor.

He was well aware when he returned to England that his relatives thought he should marry and he found himself being invited to meet innumerable attractive widows or girls who for some reason or another had not 'got off' in the first flush of their youth.

The family had waited expectantly for him to fall in love and were quite unreasonably disappointed when he did not.

His aunt had even tackled him on the subject.

"After all, Chilton," she had said, "you know as well as I do that you should now settle down and produce an heir. I always think it so much better when the title goes in a direct line."

"You can hardly say that it has come in a direct line as far as I am concerned," Lord Hawkston had replied with a smile.

"I am well aware of that," his aunt answered, "and that is why I think you should produce a son as quickly as possible."

"I have first to find a wife."

"I have been looking around for you," his aunt had said, "and, there are several ladies whom I consider suitable."

"I have an uncomfortable feeling that your plans will go awry," Lord Hawkston replied. "I have no intention. Aunt Alice, and let me make this quite clear, of marrying anyone for the sake of the title, the estate or the Family Tree."

"Now, Chilton," his aunt said sharply, "don't be so difficult, I am not suggesting that you should marry someone without affection, but you are getting a little old to be knocked head-over-heels at the sight of a pretty face."

"You are right there," Lord Hawkston smiled.

"Therefore, if I can find you a charming woman, between twenty-five and thirty, or perhaps even a little older, experienced and sophisticated, who will amuse and entertain you, then doubtless in time she will arouse a response in your heart."

The problem was, Lord Hawkston found, that the women his aunt produced aroused no response either in his heart or his mind.

He told himself that perhaps he was expecting too much and yet, although he appeared to be reserved and ruthless, there was deep inside him a longing for a love that might mean as much to him as the beauty of Ceylon.

Often, when he had stood on the verandah of his house and looked at the green mountains peaking round it towards the sky and at the torrent of crystal water rushing below him in the valley, he had felt that the sheer beauty of it evoked a response in him that was almost like the first rising of desire for a very beautiful woman.

'It is absurd to be in love with a country!' he told himself.

And yet he knew that he had grown to love Ceylon as a man might love his wife.

The loveliness, the softness, the gentleness of it, combined with the warm moist air, were everything that was feminine, everything that inspired a feeling that was almost spiritual in its intensity.

'This is what love should be,' he thought and tried to laugh at his own fantasy.

CHAPTER TWO

Lord Hawkston decided that he would speak to the Governor about his problem of finding a wife for his nephew, Gerald.

He was wondering what he would tell Sir Arthur about Emily Ludgrove, only to find the moment he opened the conversation that she had forestalled him.

Sir Arthur Gordon, a grandson of the Earl of Aberdeen, whom Lord Hawkston had known slightly before he left for England, was a man of austere dignity who inspired his subordinates with awe as well as respect.

When he had assumed charge in Ceylon in 1883, the island was still racked by the economic crisis of the coffee slump, but the tide was turning slowly and the plantations were exploring the possibilities not only of tea but also of cinchong.

Sir Arthur took a personal interest in these developments especially the establishment of the tea industry. He had sent inspectors to Loolecondera and Lord Hawkston's plantation and had been extremely impressed by their reports. He was later to visit several tea plantations himself.

Both James Taylor and Lord Hawkston liked him and found it easy to convince him that tea would bring prosperity back to Ceylon.

What Lord Hawkston particularly liked about Sir Arthur was his determination to demonstrate his impartiality to all races.

In fact just before Lord Hawkston left for England the Governor had threatened to withdraw his patronage from a European Colombo club that tried to exclude certain Ceylonese from its membership.

What endeared him even further was that he protected the interests of the village Head men and the property rights of Buddhist Temples.

He was the most enlightened and progressive Governor that Ceylon had had for many years.

He carried out the restoration of many irrigation tanks and canals, completed the Colombo Oort's breakwater, the foundation stone of which had been laid by the Prince of Wales in 1875, extended the railway and began to build an estimated two hundred and sixty miles of new roadways.

It would have been difficult for people in England, Lord Hawkston thought as he looked at him, to realise the power of a Governor of Ceylon. He not only reigned but ruled and was surrounded by all the trappings of Royalty.

He had residences in Colombo, Nuwara, Sliya, Kandy and Jaffma, he had a Ceylonese bodyguard more imposing than the Beefeaters in England and a troop of Sikh Cavalry to precede and follow him on visits of State.

A line Regiment furnished him with a guard and he had a special train for his travels.

All memoranda to the Queen passed through his hands. He had the last word and what his last word was none knew but himself.

It was impossible not to remember that Sir Arthur was an aristocrat and very conscious of his authority so that Lord Hawkston wondered how much it would be wise to tell him about Emily Ludgrove.

He decided that he would not mention her behaviour with Captain O'Neill, not because he was particularly concerned with protecting Emily's reputation, but because he liked Patrick O'Neill and felt that in choosing such a wife he would certainly have enough problems on his hands.

However, when Lord Hawkston entered the Governor's study, they were alone, the secretary having been dismissed and Sir Arthur then said with a smile,

"I know what you have come to tell me, Hawkston. Miss Ludgrove has already informed me that she wishes to marry Captain O'Neill."

Lord Hawkston did not reply and Sir Arthur went on,

"I feel this will be annoying for you, considering that you brought her out especially to marry your nephew. From all I hear the young man needs the steadying influence of a wife."

Lord Hawkston was not surprised that the Governor had so intimate knowledge of Gerald's behaviour.

He was far more astute than people realised and, although in the grandeur and splendour of the Queen's House, he seemed immune from the commonplaces of everyday life, there was little that went on not only in Colombo but also in other parts of the country that he was not aware of.

"I am afraid, Your Excellency, that my nephew has been making a fool of himself," Lord Hawkston admitted.

"It happens to a great number of young men when they first come out here," Sir Arthur answered, "and, as you and I well know, Hawkston, there are plenty of people who are only too willing to help a man sow his wild oats, especially if he has money to pay for them."

"That is true," Lord Hawkston agreed somewhat grudgingly.

He remembered certain wild nights he had experienced when he first arrived in Colombo, but he had been far too careful of his precious money to expend much of it on tawdry women and the dubious entertainments that were provided for greenhorns who had just arrived from England.

He had later, however, enjoyed a pleasant liaison with a very pretty Portuguese in Kandy whom he visited whenever he could spare the time from running his plantation. It had lasted for years, but he had been very discreet about it.

It hurt his pride now to realise that Gerald's misdemeanours were known even to the Governor.

"I wish we could have taken better care of your nephew when he first came out," Sir Arthur was saying thoughtfully. "He had several meals here, but, as you well know, hospitality in Government House is inevitably formal and must seem tedious to the young. I have learnt from my secretary that we invited him to a ball I gave at Christmas, but he did not reply to the invitation."

Lord Hawkston's lips tightened.

If there was one thing he disliked more than anything else, it was bad manners. He had thought in the short time that he had known Gerald when he was in England that he at least knew how to behave like a gentleman in public.

"Anyway the question now is," the Governor went on, "what are you going to do about him?"

"I intend, Your Excellency, to provide him with a wife," Lord Hawkston replied in a hard voice. "I came out here with the girl he had chosen for himself, but as those plans have gone awry, I must make good the deficiency by finding him someone else."

Sir Arthur laughed.

"Is not that just like you, Hawkston? You have a reputation for being undefeatable and all I can say is that

Gerald Warren is a lucky young man to have you as an uncle."

"Naturally I shall need your help, Your Excellency."

The Governor laughed again.

"I cannot believe that I can be of any real assistance. I can assure you that there is a scarcity of charming unattached young ladies in this establishment. Nevertheless it should not be difficult to find someone suitable amongst the many English families living in Colombo."

He sat down at his desk and put his hand to his forehead.

"Let me think about it. I have not really taken very much notice of the military families, but I daresay that there are one or two daughters of Officers not yet snapped up by some eager Subaltern."

"I should prefer a girl who has lived in Colombo for some time," Lord Hawkston said. "I have grown so used myself to seeing all the admirable qualities of this country that I had forgotten that people new to the rather specialised existence here might find a few snags."

"You are thinking of the loneliness of being isolated on a plantation for months on end," Sir Arthur said with a serious note in his voice. "You will have to find a very exceptional girl who will stand that sort of life, Hawkston. If you will forgive my saying so, I thought from the moment that I set eyes on Miss Ludgrove that she was not the right type."

"I see that now," Lord Hawkston agreed, "but she was Gerald's choice not mine."

"And do you think he will be prepared to accept yours without having any say in the matter?"

"He will do as he is told, unless he wishes to be sent back to England," Lord Hawkston declared. "In which case he can work his passage for I have no intention of paying it for him!"

He spoke in the ruthless determined manner that was familiar to those who worked with him.

The Governor gave him a speculative glance before he said quietly,

"Playing God where love and marriage are concerned is a tricky business, Hawkston. You may burn your fingers."

"I am listening to Your Excellency's warning," Lord Hawkston answered, "but I still need your assistance."

"I have just seen the list of the people who are dining here tonight," the Governor said, "and none of them will be of any use in this respect. All I can say is that you had best take a glance at the congregation in Church tomorrow morning."

He saw the expression on Lord Hawkston's face and added with a smile,

"You know as well as I do that if you stay in the Queen's House you are expected to accompany the Governor to Morning Prayers."

"I am quite prepared to do my duty," Lord Hawkston replied.

"It will not be as hard as you think," Sir Arthur went on. "I have restricted the Vicar to a sermon not longer than fifteen minutes!"

*

The following morning in the grey stone Church of St. Peter's, which was not far from the Queen's House, Lord

Hawkston, looking round the congregation, saw that the pews were filled with elegant figures that would have surprised those who thought that Ceylon was a backwater and out of touch with the world of fashion.

Gowns of taffeta, silk, satin, bombazine ornamented with lace, braid, buttons or ribbon were not only fashionable but luxurious.

So were the extremely fetching bonnets and hats trimmed with flowers and feathers that rested on the elegantly coiffured heads of the female worshippers.

Lord Hawkston had always heard that Sunday in Colombo was a fashion parade, but, as he had never himself attended a Service in the Capital, it surprised him to see so many European faces. He noticed that many of them were extremely attractive.

He had, however, a suspicion that the most elegantly garbed and certainly the most sophisticated were the wives of Army Officers or Government Officials.

Behind the European congregation with an aisle between them sat the Ceylonese, even more resplendent in their colourful saris, their silks and cottons dyed by using the wax-resistant handicraft process that was, Lord Hawkston knew, a speciality of local weavers.

The rich and exotic colours and materials, ranging from the simplest gossamer to glittering embroidery, made the Ceylonese worshippers look like a bouquet of flowers against the grey stone of the Church walls.

The Governor had been met at the Church door by the Vicar in his surplice and escorted in the traditional manner to his stall in the Chancel, where there were comfortable velvet cushions and prayer books emblazoned with the British Coat of Arms.

Opposite the Governor's stall were the seats for the choir and behind them an organ which, Lord Hawkston noticed as the Service began, was played by a young woman wearing a white cotton dress and an ugly black bonnet tied with black ribbons.

She looked, he thought, very austere compared with the other women in the congregation. Then he noticed with surprise that her dress was duplicated by five other figures seated at the back of the choir stalls.

All five wore identical white cotton dresses, black bonnets and black gloves and their waists were encircled with narrow black sashes.

He thought at first that it must be a special costume for choir women, but, as he stared at them, he heard the Governor whisper in his ear,

"The Vicar has six daughters!"

"Six?" Lord Hawkston nearly exclaimed aloud.

"His wife died two years ago," the Governor said behind his Prayer Book. "It has made him even more intent on making us aware of our sins and the hell fires that await us."

Lord Hawkston looked at the Vicar with interest. He was a thin gaunt man who might have been good-looking in his youth. But now, painfully thin and cadaverous, he gave the impression of a man who had crushed out of himself all the pleasures of life.

There was a fanatical look about him, Lord Hawkston decided, and he wondered whether his daughters suffered from what, he was quite certain, was a stern rigidity and self-imposed privation.

He then looked at the girls with renewed interest.

The oldest of those sitting facing him had a rather pretty face, as far as he could see under the brim of her bonnet.

The others, who were obviously not yet grown up, had pink-and-white complexions, small turned up noses and large curious eyes that stared unblinkingly at the congregation.

The oldest member of the family, who played the organ, seemed to have eyes in the back of her head. As her youngest sister was fidgeting, she turned quickly to reprove her, at the same time handing to a small Ceylonese choirboy an open prayer book when he had obviously become hopelessly lost in finding the right place on his own.

When she was not playing the organ, the older girl turned round so that she could watch the behaviour of the choir.

'Obviously a very competent young woman,' Lord Hawkston thought to himself as he saw her once again open a prayer book and hand it to another small boy who had no idea what responses he should be making.

When she rose from her place, he could see that she had a slim elegant figure, which surprisingly was not entirely disguised by the coarse cotton that her dress was made of.

Having lived for so long in Ceylon, Lord Hawkston was well aware that the gowns worn by the Vicar's daughters were made of the cheapest white material that was used only by the poorest Ceylonese.

The Governor had said that their mother had died two years ago. This meant that either the Vicar insisted on the long and tedious mourning that had become fashionable in England or else, since their bonnets were not yet worn out, they would continue to wear them until it was absolutely imperative to purchase new ones.

The choir rose to sing a psalm and Lord Hawkston realised that despite the age of the organ it was being played skilfully. The Vicar's oldest daughter was definitely something of a musician.

All through the Service he found himself speculating about the family and wondering what their lives were like.

He had a better idea of the atmosphere that they had been brought up in as he listened to the Vicar's sermon.

There was no doubt that the Governor was right and the man was obsessed with the idea of sin and with the punishment that would be inflicted on all sinners from which there was no escape.

He spoke with a zeal that was unmistakable and a fire that came from the deep sincerity of conviction.

As a Priest he was undoubtedly dedicated, but as a father, Lord Hawkston mused, he must be hard to endure.

The Vicar faltered once in his sermon when he must inadvertently have turned over two pages of his notes at the same time.

When he did so, his eldest daughter turned her head quickly to look up at the pulpit and Lord Hawkston saw her face completely for the first time.

It was heart-shaped with a small straight nose and large eyes, which appeared to Lord Hawkston, at the distance he was from her, to be grey.

Her eyebrows were arched almost like the wings of a bird against an oval forehead and he guessed that beneath the black bonnet her hair, which was almost ash in colour, was drawn back tightly and unbecomingly.

The Vicar found his place and his daughter seemed to relax. She turned her head once again to see what was going on amongst the choir and bent forward to admonish a small boy who was playing with a catapult.

He had drawn it from his pocket beneath his surplice and, startled by her attention, dropped the catapult and the stone that he was intending to use in its sling.

It fell to the ground with a thud and the Vicar's daughter bent forward with the obvious intention of telling him to leave it where it was until after the Service was over, but she was too late.

Frightened at losing his most treasured possession, the choirboy was crawling about amongst the legs of the two boys who sat on either side of him in an effort to retrieve his treasures.

He found them and slipped back on to the seat giving an anguished look at the Vicar's daughter as he did so.

She frowned at him. Then, as he bent his head in contrition, she caught the eye of her sister and gave her a faintly amused smile.

It completely transformed the solemnity of her face and at that moment Lord Hawkston made up his mind.

This was the right type of wife for Gerald, he told himself, a girl who could cope with a fanatical father, a collection of naughty choirboys and a household full of sisters and would undoubtedly be able to manage his nephew in a most competent manner.

The idea was certainly worth exploring and he could not help feeling that this was far better material to work on for the reclamation of his nephew than the other women in the congregation rustling self-consciously in silks and satins and obviously paying no attention to the Vicar's strictures.

"Tell me about your Parson," Lord Hawkston said as he drove back at the Governor's side towards Queen's House in a carriage pulled by two excellent horses.

"He is a difficult chap," Sir Arthur replied. "He is always complaining to me about the iniquities that go on round the Port and other less savoury parts of the town. I have to explain to him that it is not the Governor's job to prevent men spending their money as they wish and, unless they are breaking the law, I have no jurisdiction to interfere."

"What about his family?" Lord Hawkston enquired.

"I hardly know them," the Governor replied. "They are invited to various entertainments from time to time, but their father mourns his wife in a manner that precludes everything, I suspect, except prayer. So we only see the eldest girl when there are meetings regarding the Church school or at fundraising occasions for the work that the Vicar does amongst the poor."

"It sounds a gloomy existence."

"I should imagine most young women today would find it completely intolerable," the Governor agreed.

"I was reading," Lord Hawkston remarked, "that the spread of Christianity and education among the people of Ceylon is greater than in any other Eastern state."

"I think that is true," Sir Arthur replied. "On the last census we had two hundred and twenty thousand Roman Catholics, fifty thousand Protestants and about two million Buddhists."

He paused to add with a twinkle in his eyes,

"Other occupations of our people include one thousand five hundred devil dancers, one hundred and twenty-one snake charmers, six hundred and forty tom-tom beaters, five thousand fakirs and devotee beggars!"

Lord Hawkston laughed.

"A mixed bag!"

There was no time to say more, as the carriage had drawn up at the Queen's House.

After luncheon Lord Hawkston sought out the Governor's Secretary, an elderly man who had spent all his life in Colombo.

He had served successive Governors who found his knowledge of local affairs invaluable.

"I want to know all you can tell me about the Vicar of St. Peter's," Lord Hawkston asked him.

"His name is Radford," the Secretary replied. "He has been in Colombo for twenty-two years. He married out here and he is quite convinced that in the Queen's House we are a callous unfeeling lot who have no sympathy with his violent desire to clean up the City of Colombo."

"He should compare it with other coastal Cities of the same size," Lord Hawkston said dryly. "He would be surprised to find that in contrast Colombo is, in my opinion at any rate, an exemplary example of good behaviour."

"I would not go as far as to say that, my Lord, but there is in fact very little vice and on the whole our people are well behaved."

"That is what I have always thought myself. And now tell me about Mrs. Radford."

"She was a charming, lady," the Secretary answered. "If anyone could keep the Vicar human, it was his wife. She came from a County family in England and her father was concerned with the Botanical Gardens at Kew. She came out with him when he was advising the Governor of the time on certain plants and trees that would do well in our particular soil. She met the Vicar, he was only a Curate in those days, and fell in love with him."

The Secretary paused before adding,

"When I knew Radford first, he was an attractive young man, but even then fired with a prophetic zeal that I had always thought would be extremely uncomfortable to live with."

"They had six daughters?"

"It has always been a deep sorrow to the Vicar that he had no son," the Secretary explained. "After Miss Dominica and Miss Faith were born he christened his third daughter Hope, but unfortunately she was followed by three more sisters – Miss Charity, Miss Grace and Miss Prudence!"

"Good Heavens!" Lord Hawkston cried. "What names to saddle poor girls with for the rest of their lives!"

"Dominica was lucky," the Secretary continued. "She was born on a Sunday and therefore it seemed a suitable choice, but for the others it is another cross they have to bear."

"I can well imagine that," Lord Hawkston remarked.

"They are all very pleasant girls," the Secretary said. "My wife thinks very highly of them and occasionally they are allowed to come to tea with my daughter, who is an invalid. Otherwise they have few amusements. Their father does not approve of secular interests."

"I wish to call on the Vicar," Lord Hawkston declared. "May I mention your name by way of introduction?"

The Secretary smiled.

"Mention the Governor's, my Lord. Despite himself, the Vicar is impressed by His Excellency."

"I will take your advice," Lord Hawkston replied.

He called at the Vicarage at four o'clock in the afternoon, feeling that it was not only the correct social time for calling but it would also undoubtedly be between Services.

The door was opened by one of the sisters who looked about fourteen years old and whom he suspected was Charity.

She gave him a startled glance and, when he explained that he wished to see her father, she ushered him in a somewhat embarrassed manner into the front room of the Vicarage, saying that she would fetch him.

Lord Hawkston looked around and realised that everything was poor but at the same time tasteful.

The curtain material could not have cost more than a few pence a yard, yet they were skilfully made and in a colour that echoed the blue of the sea.

There were, however, no sofa cushions and the floor, scrubbed until it literally shone with cleanliness, was covered by only a few cheap native mats. The whitewashed walls were bare except for one landscape in water colours.

There was a bowl of flowers on a plain table by the fireplace and the room smelt of pot-pourri, which after a moment Lord Hawkston located in a bowl set on the window ledge where ordinarily it would catch the rays of the sun.

But since it was Sunday the blinds were lowered until only a foot of light came from the bottom of each window.

Lord Hawkston knew that it was customary in Scotland and in some of the country parts of England to pull down the blinds on the Sabbath, but it was something that he had not expected to find in Ceylon.

He realised, however, when the Vicar appeared that he had in fact committed a transgression by calling on a Sunday.

"You wish to see me?" the Vicar asked coming into the room and looking, Lord Hawkston thought, even more gaunt and austere than he had seemed in Church.

The sombre black of his clothing, the sharpness of his cheekbones, the thinness of his face and the grey of his hair, which was almost white at the temples, made him look like one of the ancient prophets ready to cry doom on the inhabitants of Sodom and Gomorrah.

"I am Lord Hawkston!"

The Vicar made a small inclination of his head.

"I am staying at Queen's House with the Governor," Lord Hawkston went on. "I called, Vicar, because I need your help and because I have something of importance to discuss with you."

*

Outside the sitting room Charity closed the door behind her father and sped up the stairs.

Dominica was in her bedroom, which she shared with Faith. She was taking off her bonnet, having just returned from the Sunday school that she held immediately after luncheon.

Charity burst into the room and she looked up in surprise.

"Dominica what do you think? What do you think?"

"What has happened? Why are you so excited?" Dominica asked her.

"A gentleman has called to see Papa and he has come in one of the Governor's carriages. It's the same gentleman who was in Church today. You must have seen him he was sitting next to the Governor and I saw him look amused when Ranil dropped his catapult."

"It was not at all amusing," Dominica said. "Papa heard the noise and was very angry about it. It is difficult to make him understand that the choirboys never listen to his sermons."

"Why should they?" Charity asked lightly. "I bet the Governor does not listen either."

"I wonder what his guest wants with Papa?" Dominica said.

"He is very distinguished-looking," Charity told her, "but I don't suppose he has come to invite us to a ball."

"Charity!" Dominica exclaimed and then laughed. "You know that is as unlikely as if we had all been invited to stay on the moon! Anyway Papa would not allow us to go."

"When I am grown up like you and Faith," Charity asserted, "I shall dance whatever Papa says."

"Then you had better not let him hear you saying it now," a voice said from the doorway, "or he will give you a good whipping!"

Faith came into the bedroom as she spoke and Lord Hawkston had been right in thinking that she was a very pretty girl.

Without the ugly black bonnet that had overshadowed her face she had fair hair, blue eyes and an almost angelic expression, but she also, although it did not show in her face, had a mischievous wit and was, like Charity, ready to rebel against the restrictions imposed upon them by their father.

"What is all this?" Faith asked now. "Is it true there is a young man in the house?"

"He is not particularly young," Charity answered, "but he is smart and very impressive and he is staying at Queen's House."

"Is he the one who was in Church today?" Faith asked.

Charity nodded.

"I had a good look at him," Faith said, "and thought he was rather attractive."

Dominica laughed.

"You would find any man attractive, Faith, as well you know."

"I don't have the chance to see many except in Church," Faith retorted. "I hoped that Lieutenant who made eyes at me last Sunday would be there today, but he must be on duty. There was no sign of him."

Dominica glanced towards the door.

"Do be careful, Faith," she begged. "I am always afraid that Papa will hear you talking like that."

"Papa is far too busy looking for sin in the town to ferret it out in his own household," Faith replied lightly.

"I should not be too sure of that," Dominica warned her.

"What do you think the gentleman downstairs is talking about to Papa?" Charity said. "Shall I listen at the door? If Papa found me in the hall, I could say I was waiting to show his guest out."

"Yes, do that," Faith agreed quickly.

But Dominica interposed,

"You will do nothing of the sort, Charity. It is vulgar and ill-bred to listen at keyholes, as well you know."

"But why do you think he wishes to see Papa?" Charity asked.

"We shall know in good time," Dominica answered calmly.

Then she gave a little cry.

"Heavens, do you think he will stay to tea? I meant to make a cake yesterday, but there was no time and also, to tell the truth, I had run out of housekeeping money and did not dare to ask Papa for any more."

"Never mind," Faith said, "we can cut him some sandwiches and Charity can collect some fruit from the garden. I expect he has stuffed himself with exotic luxuries at Queen's House and will not care for the peasant fare we have in this house."

"Faith, please don't talk like that in front of the younger ones," Dominica said almost pleadingly. "You know as well as I do that Papa thinks too much luxury incites sinful thoughts."

"Judging by what we eat," Faith replied, "it's a wonder we can think at all. I am quite certain I am suffering from malnutrition!"

Dominica laughed.

"You don't look like it! The last dress I made you had to have another inch in the waist."

"That," Faith said with dignity, "was only natural growth!"

Dominica was about to reply when she heard a voice calling to her.

"Dominica please come here, I want you."

It was her father and she looked at her sisters in consternation.

"For goodness' sake cut some sandwiches," she said quickly to Faith. "And you, Charity, find fruit of some sort and fill the wicker bowl with it. It looks nice even if the fruit is not very exciting. We finished the only ripe pawpaw yesterday."

She was still giving instructions as she opened the bedroom door and ran down the stairs.

"You are keeping me waiting, Dominica," her father called out reprovingly.

"I am sorry, Papa, I was just telling Faith and Charity what to do in case your visitor stays to tea."

"To tea?" the Vicar repeated, looking as if he had never heard of such a meal. "Yes, yes, of course. Perhaps it would be polite to offer him a cup."

"Shall I go and get it ready, Papa?"

"No, the others can do that. Lord Hawkston wishes to speak to *you.*"

Dominica looked surprised, but before she could say anything her father had opened the sitting room door and she walked into the room.

She had, of course, noticed the stranger in the Governor's pew, but she had reproved her sisters so often for looking about them curiously that she had trained herself not to look at the congregation and most of all not to stare at the worshippers from Queen's House.

Nevertheless she recognised the man she had seen opposite her in the Chancel and thought that he was even better looking than he had appeared in Church.

He was also extremely elegant in Dominica's eyes.

She never met the young Army officers who Faith cast longing eyes on, but occasionally she came in contact with the sons of the Civil Servants and other English dignitaries who resided in Ceylon.

When she did, they always seemed to her to be somewhat self-conscious in their best clothes and high white collars, almost as if they were wearing fancy dress that they were not accustomed to.

But she noticed that Lord Hawkston's clothes, smart though they were, seemed to be a part of him.

He wore them casually and yet she was well aware that they had an elegance that proclaimed all too clearly that they had been tailored in London.

He was standing at the far end of the room as she entered and she was conscious that, as she entered the room, he watched her from under his eyebrows as she walked across towards him.

The Vicar accompanied her.

"This, my Lord, is my daughter, Dominica."

Lord Hawkston bowed and Dominica swept him a low curtsey. There was a moment's silence and Dominica wondered why neither of the men spoke.

She had the feeling, perhaps erroneously, that they were feeling for words.

At last her father, clearing his throat, began,

"Lord Hawkston, Dominica, has brought me an unexpected and rather strange proposition and he has asked that you too should listen to what he has to say."

Dominica raised her grey eyes to her father's face.

"Yes, Papa?"

Again there was a pause. Then almost as if he found the situation uncomfortable Lord Hawkston said,

"I wonder, Vicar, if you would think it very unconventional if I talk with your daughter alone? I feel that I would like to make my proposition, as you call it, to her myself."

There was an expression of relief on the Vicar's face as he replied,

"Of course, my Lord. Perhaps that would be best. I will go and tell my other daughters to prepare tea."

"Thank you," Lord Hawkston nodded.

The Vicar went from the room closing the door behind him and Dominica looked at Lord Hawkston apprehensively.

She could not imagine what he wished to say to her or what he could possibly have to propose.

"Suppose we sit down?" Lord Hawkston suggested and the words brought a flush to Dominica's cheeks.

"I-I am sorry, my Lord.," she said quickly. "I should have invited you to do so, but I was so surprised to see you that – I am afraid I forgot my manners."

"I think what I have to say to you will come as an even greater surprise," Lord Hawkston replied, "but I want you to listen to me and not make up your mind too quickly."

He seated himself as he spoke on the hard sofa that stood against one wall and he made a little gesture with his hand and after a second's hesitation Dominica seated herself beside him.

He turned a little sideways to look at her and she felt uncomfortably that he was looking her over in a scrutinising manner that she did not understand.

She had, as Lord Hawkston had suspected, ash-coloured hair with faint silver lights in it. Drawn back from her forehead it was pinned tight into a large bun, which covered the whole back of her head, making him realise that her hair was long and thick.

Her eyes were grey and fringed with dark lashes and the winged eyebrows he had noticed in Church were dark too.

But her skin was translucently fair and very pale so that when she blushed it brought a sudden beauty to her face, almost like the dawn creeping up the morning sky.

She was very thin, but despite the coarse cotton of her gown it was moulded so tightly to her figure that the soft mature swellings of her breasts were easy to discern and her waist was very small and could in fact, Lord Hawkston thought, be spanned by a man's two hands.

Her fingers, which had played the ancient organ so skilfully, were long and elegant and she placed them now in her lap, almost like a child in school waiting to recite a poem.

"I expect," Lord Hawkston said at length in his deep voice, "you are wondering why I have called on your father?"

"We seldom have visitors on a Sunday."

"I apologise for desecrating the Sabbath," Lord Hawkston replied with a hint of amusement in his voice. "But my excuse is a feeling of urgency to meet you and explain to your father what I require of you."

"Of me?" Dominica asked.

"This may sound very blunt," Lord Hawkston said with his eyes on her face, "but I came here to ask your father whether you would consider marrying my nephew, Gerald Warren."

Dominica made no movement. Only her eyes widened a little as she stared at Lord Hawkston incredulously.

After a moment she said in a voice that seemed to him to be deliberately controlled,

"Is your Lordship – serious?"

"Completely!" he replied. "But let me make myself a little more explicit. My nephew, who has been working on my plantation near Kandy, has been in this country for two years. I arrived the day before yesterday with a young lady from England who he has been secretly engaged to. They were to be married on her arrival, but unfortunately when we reached Colombo I learnt that the young lady in question had changed her mind."

"Why did she now not wish – to marry him?" Dominica enquired.

"She met someone she preferred on board the ship," Lord Hawkston explained, "but anyway I am quite certain that she would not have made my nephew a commendable wife."

Dominica did not speak and after a moment he continued,

"My nephew needs someone to look after him, to give him companionship and relieve the tedium and loneliness that I am sure you will realise is experienced by planters when they are up-country for months on end."

He paused and then added,

"When I saw you in Church playing the organ so well, coping with the misdemeanours of the choirboys and at the same time giving your father your attention, I felt sure that you are the person I was looking for."

Dominica drew in her breath.

"How can you be – sure of that, my Lord?"

Lord Hawkston smiled.

"Shall I say I have an instinct for doing the right thing? I survived the coffee slump because I had been fortunate enough to plant some acres of tea on my plantation. It is now a flourishing and lucrative concern. But should my nephew not wish to make his home in Ceylon, I am sure that in a few years it would be possible for you to return to England."

There was another pause and then Dominica said,

"You said just now that you arrived on Friday and that you had expected your nephew to marry the young lady you brought from England – as soon as you reached here. Was he not very upset that his intended bride – had changed her mind?"

Lord Hawkston liked the way she had worked out for herself the significance of what had occurred and was certain that he had been right in thinking her intelligent and this was the proof of it.

"You are quite right to ask that question, Miss Radford," he said. "I will be frank with you and say that my nephew has as yet no idea that there has been a change of plan. As it happens he is ill and was unable to meet us in Colombo. I received a letter from him saying that he hopes to meet me in Kandy in a few days."

"And will you tell him then that – as he cannot have the bride he wanted you have chosen – someone else for him?"

The question was spoken softly, but Lord Hawkston could not help thinking that spoken in another tone it could have sounded sarcastic.

"I think when Gerald realises that he has escaped a very unhappy marriage and meets you he will be quite satisfied with the arrangements that I wish to make for you both."

Dominica turned her face away to look towards the light coining in through the half-closed blinds.

Lord Hawkston could see her in profile and realised that her bone structure was good.

Attractively dressed and with a less austere hairstyle, he told himself that she would be very pretty.

"Are you seriously – expecting me, my Lord, to say that I will marry a man – I have never met?" Dominica asked after a moment.

"I am asking you to trust me," Lord Hawkston answered, "when I tell you that my nephew is a good-looking young man, in fact I have been told that some women find him handsome. He is nearly six feet tall, a hard rider to hounds when in England, and is, I believe, equally at home on the dance floor."

"Supposing he – dislikes me?" Dominica asked in a low voice.

"I think in the circumstances he is living now he will welcome with open arms the companionship of an attractive girl who will have his interests at heart and who will make his life comfortable and pleasant."

Lord Hawkston paused for a moment to continue,

"After all, supposing you had met him two or three times? Supposing you had danced with him? That would constitute enough acquaintanceship for him to ask you to marry him and for you to accept. All I am asking is for you to dispense with such trivial formalities and agree to be his wife, trusting me to have described him fairly."

Dominica did not reply and after a moment Lord Hawkston went on,

"I am sure it has not escaped your notice that your father, having six daughters, may find it difficult to provide suitable husbands for them all. If you marry my nephew, I intend to settle an adequate amount of money for your comfort and there will be much more when I die."

Dominica glanced at him swiftly.

"That will surely not be for a long time, my Lord."

Lord Hawkston smiled.

"I am approaching middle-age and let me assure you that I have no intention of marrying. I have lived alone for so long and have become so used to my own company that I am content to remain a bachelor. In which case Gerald will eventually inherit the title and the family estates and property in England, which are considerable."

Dominica looked away from him again.

And after a moment she said,

"Mama always said it was – unlucky to wait for dead men's shoes."

"But I have promised that you will be comfortable before I am dead."

She did not turn to look at him and after a moment he went on,

"I have chosen you, Dominica, and I hope you will allow me to call you by your Christian name because when I watched you in Church I felt that you were sensible. I hope you will apply that good sense to this proposition."

He watched her face as he spoke, liking the sensitiveness and the true calmness of her expression.

"I know it is unusual," he went on, "unconventional if you like, but I see no reason why you should refuse it on that account. Let me take you to Kandy and up to my plantation. When you meet my nephew, I am sure that you will find you have a great deal in common with each other."

His voice ceased and Dominica rose from the sofa and walked very slowly across the room.

She pulled up the blind on one of the windows and looked out into the garden.

Sunshine flooded in and Lord Hawkston saw her silhouetted against the golden splendour of it.

She stared out with what he guessed were unseeing eyes.

"What is worrying you?" he asked at length.

"I was thinking – about Mama," Dominica answered, "and wondering what she would – advise me to say."

"I think your mother would wish you to marry," Lord Hawkston responded. "Your father tells me that you are over twenty and most girls of that age are already thinking of a bridal veil."

"Mama was only eighteen – when she married," Dominica replied, "but she fell very much in love with Papa – as soon as she saw him."

"As I am certain that you will fall in love with my nephew," Lord Hawkston said.

Dominica made no response and after a moment he went on,

"Let me ask you once again to be sensible about this. I have heard that your father does not allow you and your sisters to attend many social functions. How do you suppose any of you will get married if you never meet men and if you are not allowed to go to dances and parties?"

He stopped for a moment and then resumed.

"Do you really envisage living on indefinitely in this house in the years ahead, looking after your sisters and your father, controlling the choirboys, and teaching, as I hear you have been doing this afternoon, in Sunday school? What sort of life is that?"

"I think Mama would have wanted us to have some – gaiety," Dominica said slowly, "and to meet many more people than we do now, but it angers and upsets Papa when I suggest it."

Suddenly she turned round to face Lord Hawkston.

"You would not like Faith to marry your nephew?" she asked. "Faith is longing to be married. She wants to meet men and I am sure that she would be very happy to agree to your proposition."

Lord Hawkston shook his head.

"Faith, as your father told me, is only just eighteen and I have a feeling that she has not your good sense nor your intelligence. Anyway I have made up my mind. I want *you*, Dominica. I want you to agree to travel with me to Kandy as soon as we have bought your trousseau."

"Trousseau!"

The exclamation came from Dominica's lips sharply.

Then before Lord Hawkston could speak she said quickly,

"You must understand, my Lord, it would be impossible for me to have many more gowns – than I already possess or to expend much money on buying new things. Papa would never allow it and besides the money – is not there. You must realise that we are very poor."

"I am well aware of that," Lord Hawkston replied, "and I promise you, Dominica, that you shall have a delightful trousseau, the best that Colombo can provide and it will not cost your father a penny."

"Do you mean that you will pay – for it?"

"Most certainly!"

"But I don't think Papa – " Dominica began hesitatingly.

"Leave your father to me," Lord Hawkston urged her. "As I have already told you, Dominica, I always get my own way. I can easily persuade your father that as far as a trousseau is concerned my way is the best."

His eyes were on her face as he went on,

"My way is also best where you are concerned. Will you not be content, Dominica, to leave everything in my hands and to let me make the arrangements I think fit? I am quite certain you will never regret it."

"How can you be – certain?"

"I have pointed out the alternative," Lord Hawkston replied. "Would it not be better to be the wife of a charming, pleasant young man with a certain amount of money and the prospect of a great deal more, than a future when you will become a frustrated old maid slaving to make ends meet and finding that your efforts seldom evoke much appreciation?"

This was a shrewd thrust that he knew went home.

He had already realised from the talk that he had had with the Vicar that he had very little idea of how much his daughter did and was not in the least grateful for her efforts to keep the house going now that his wife was dead.

Lord Hawkston's eyes took in all the indecision he could see in Dominica's face and he knew that his arguments were, although she made little sign of it, causing a sense of chaos within her mind so that it was hard for her to think clearly.

Because he was used to leading men and getting from them exactly what he wanted Lord Hawkston applied the same technique to Dominica.

"Come," he said in a kindly tone. "You have everything to gain and nothing to lose. Give me your hand and tell me that your answer is 'yes'."

He held out his hand as he spoke and hesitatingly, because he expected it of her, Dominica laid her fingers on his. He could feel that they were very cold and they trembled a little.

"Your answer is 'yes', is it not?" Lord Hawkston insisted.

"Yes – my Lord," Dominica answered, but her voice was hardly above a whisper.

CHAPTER THREE

Lord Hawkston did not wait for the tea that had been prepared for him with so much trouble.

He had learnt in the business world that having concluded a difficult negotiation it was always wise to leave before the other party began to regret that he had accepted the proposition and wished to change his mind.

"Don't disturb your father," he said to Dominica. "I will leave now, but I will return tomorrow morning and arrange to take you shopping for your trousseau,"

Dominica did not answer and he knew that she felt as if her voice had died in her throat.

"I am very grateful to you," Lord Hawkston said, "for agreeing to marry my nephew."

He bowed, Dominica curtseyed and opened the front door for him.

The Governor's carriage, emblazoned with the British Coat of Arms, its fine horses and silver accoutrements, was looking very resplendent outside the shabby Vicarage.

Dominica could not help feeling that the servants in their elaborate livery looked disdainfully at their surroundings.

A footman opened the door of the open carriage for Lord Hawkston and he stepped into it. Having put a light rug over his Lordship's knees to keep off the dust, the footman sprang up onto the box and the horses started off.

Lord Hawkston raised his high hat and Dominica curtseyed again.

She stood watching the carriage until it was out of sight and did not know that Lord Hawkston had liked the way she stood quite still, her head held a little defiantly as if she summoned some inner courage to her aid.

'A very sensible girl,' he told himself as he drove away. 'She will be the saving of Gerald and undoubtedly they will deal very well together.'

When there was no longer any sign of the carriage on the unkempt Vicarage drive, Dominica walked back into the house, closed the door and stood for a moment leaning against it as if she needed to support herself against a sudden weakness.

Then she ran into the kitchen at the back of the house where she would find her sisters.

They were all there, Faith was cutting sandwiches and Charity and Hope were arranging the fruit in a wicker basket.

They had been chattering as Dominica entered the room, but immediately they fell silent as they all turned their faces towards her, a question in their eyes.

"What did he want?" Charity asked at once.

Faith, throwing down the butter knife, exclaimed,

"You don't mean to say he has gone without the tea we are taking so much trouble over! How could you let him go, Dominica, when we all wanted to see him?"

"He has gone," Dominica answered in a strange voice and walking to the table she sat down on one of the hard chairs.

"What did he come about?" Hope enquired.

She was not as pretty as Faith, but she had the same blue eyes and golden hair. She was, however, at sixteen, going through a tomboy stage and her hair was invariably untidy and her fingernails dirty.

"Yes, what did he want?" Charity repeated impatiently.

"He has asked me to marry – his nephew!"

Dominica knew that at first they did not believe her. Then, as if the quiet seriousness of her voice convinced them, they stared at her wide-eyed and astonished to the point of what might have seemed ludicrous were Dominica not experiencing the same feeling herself.

"He has asked you to do *what*?" Faith said at last.

"To marry his nephew," Dominica replied. "He is a tea planter and the girl whom Lord Hawkston brought out to marry him – "

She got no further.

"*Lord* Hawkston?" Charity exclaimed. "Do you mean to say he is a Lord?"

"A Lord!" Faith interposed. "And he actually came here to the house. Oh, Dominica, how could you have let him go?"

"He is coming back tomorrow – to buy my trousseau for me."

There was a babble that made it impossible to distinguish anything anyone was saying. The words *trousseau*, *Lord* and *marriage*, seemed to be repeated over and over again and jumbled into a roar of sound that made Dominica finally put her hands over her ears and cry,

"Stop! I must think. I must be certain I have done the – right thing."

"If you really mean you are going to marry the nephew of a Lord, I cannot imagine that you have anything to think about," Faith said. "It's the most exciting, thrilling thing I have ever heard!"

"Of course it is," Hope exclaimed. "We can all come and stay with you. Do you think he would lend me a horse to ride? And there is fishing up in the mountains where the tea grows. I would not be any trouble. You will ask me, Dominica?"

"She will have us all to stay," Faith answered as Dominica did not speak, "but leave her alone now. Give her a cup of tea, Charity. Dominica, eat one of these sandwiches. They are quite nice and you ate practically nothing at luncheon."

"There wasn't much to eat," Grace joined in.

She was small, fat and greedy and was always complaining that she did not have enough food.

"Well, you don't go hungry at any rate," Hope said sharply. "You never do."

"Stop squabbling, you two," Faith asserted. "Can't you see that Dominica is upset?"

She put two sandwiches on a plate as she spoke and put them down in front of Dominica and Charity set a cup of tea beside her.

"Drink it up," she said encouragingly, "and then you can tell us all about it."

Prudence, the youngest, who was only nine, went to stand beside her oldest sister.

"Don't leave us, Dominica," she said in a pleading voice. "We'll never be able to manage without you."

Dominica put her arm round the child and drew her close.

"That is what I am afraid of," she answered. "Oh, girls, have I made the right decision? When I said I would do as Lord Hawkston proposed, I thought that I would be able to help all of you."

"We can come to stay," Hope said irrepressibly.

"And you can give us all your cast-off clothes," Faith suggested.

"I expect he has lots of money," Charity remarked. "Lords are very rich."

Dominica took a sip of the tea and then, as if it sustained her, she went on,

"Lord Hawkston said that if I would marry his nephew he would give us enough money to be comfortable. I will be able to help you and I must somehow persuade Papa that you will need Mallika to come in every day to do the housework and not just once a week as she does now."

"She will have to help with the cooking," Faith said quickly. "You know how bad I am at it. The stove will never work for me."

"But will Papa agree?" Dominica asked. "I am sure I ought to have said 'no'. Besides it must be wrong to marry a man you have never seen."

"I expect he is tall and handsome like his uncle," Charity came in, "and when he sees you, Dominica, he will fall madly in love with you and you with him. It will be just like a fairy story."

Dominica put down her cup and rose from the table.

"I don't believe it's true!" she cried. "Did Lord Hawkston really come to the house – or have I dreamt it all?"

"It's true! It's true!" Charity cried. "I let him in! I fetched Papa and think, Dominica, how exciting it will be to have a Wedding in the family! Is Papa going to marry you?"

Dominica looked at her sister with troubled eyes.

"I don't think so," she replied. "I believe Lord Hawkston means to take me up to Kandy and I shall be married there."

"Then we cannot be bridesmaids," Faith exclaimed in a tone of disappointment. "Oh, Dominica, I do want to be your bridesmaid."

"Why has the young man, whatever his name is, not come to Colombo to meet his uncle?" Hope asked.

"He is ill," Dominica answered, "and his name is Gerald Warren."

"I think Gerald is quite a romantic name," Charity murmured.

"Warren is rather dull," Faith said, "Mrs. Warren, well, I suppose it sounds all right. It's a pity he is not a Lord too."

"He will be one day, if his uncle does not marry – and he says he intends to remain a bachelor," Dominica said in a low voice.

All three older girls gave a cry of sheer excitement and Charity exclaimed,

"You will be a Lady! Think of it, Dominica! You will be a Lady and sit on the right of the Governor when you dine at Queen's House."

For the first time since she had come into the kitchen Dominica smiled.

"That possibility is a long way ahead. After all Lord Hawkston is not old."

"I thought in Church that he looked about thirty-five or thirty-six," Faith said. "I am rather good at guessing ages."

"I thought he was much older than that," Charity contradicted her sister. "But he looks distinguished. I would like to see him with a coronet on his head."

"I don't suppose he travels with it," Dominica said with a smile.

"What else did he – ?" Faith began, then the bell on the wall pealed and there was a sudden silence.

"Papa," Faith exclaimed. "Charity, go and see what he wants."

"No, I will go," Dominica interposed. "I am sure he wants me."

There was no protest against her answering her father's summons. All the girls, with the exception of Dominica, were afraid of their father and even the thought of him was enough to change the subject of their conversation and the tone of their voices.

Dominica walked to the kitchen table and picking up her cup of tea drank from it. Then, as if it made her feel stronger, she went from the kitchen without another word.

She walked along the narrow rambling passage that led to the front of the house.

The Vicarage had been built fifty years earlier in the grandiose Colonial manner, which had given the first Vicar who had lived in it a background of pomp and consequence.

He had, however, been a rich man while the incumbents of St. Peter's who followed him were poor and without private means to supplement the very modest stipend they were allocated by the Church Commissioners in England.

Only Dominica and her mother before her knew how hard it was to keep such a big building clean, but she accepted the work that it entailed as part of her daily life and made no complaints.

The Vicar's study was an enormous room overlooking the garden and, while the best pieces of furniture they possessed were arranged there, they still seemed sparse and miserably inadequate.

The Vicar was sitting at his desk and, when Dominica entered, closing the door behind her, he said sharply,

"Why did you not fetch me to say 'goodbye' to Lord Hawkston?"

"He did not wish to stay to tea, Papa," Dominica answered, "and he will be calling again tomorrow."

"He told you what he proposed?"

"Yes, Papa."

"I accepted his proposition because I thought it was best for you, Dominica. After all, as his Lordship pointed out to me, I have six daughters who will all doubtless require husbands in the future."

"Yes, Papa."

"I would have wished to see the young man for myself, but Lord Hawkston speaks well of his nephew and I know your mother, Dominica, would have been glad for you to marry an Englishman who has not been corrupted by the sin and depravity which I find so prevalent in this country."

"Yes, Papa."

"Lord Hawkston has told you of his plans? That he should take you to Kandy and that you should be married there?"

"I would have wished you to marry me, Papa."

"It is what I had always hoped to do. But you know as well as I do, Dominica, that I cannot spare the time and, what is more, I could not contemplate the expense."

"No, of course not, Papa."

"I will give you my Blessing before you leave," the Vicar said. "And now, Dominica, I think we should both pray that you will have God's help to sustain you in your new life and that you will not fall short of the ideals and standards that I have instilled in you since you were a child."

As he spoke, the Vicar dropped to his knees beside his desk.

Dominica knelt down on the floor in front of it.

They were all used to their father praying at any time of the day that occurred to him besides taking part in the long Service of prayers he conducted every morning and every evening.

Dominica was not the least self-conscious and, kneeling on the floor without any support, she clasped her hands together and closed her eyes.

As her father burst into a long exhortation to the Almighty to preserve her from sin and temptation, Dominica said her own prayers, which were far simpler and indeed more comforting.

'Help me, God, to be sure that I have done the right thing,' she prayed, 'and that Mama would have approved. It seems strange and somehow wrong to marry a man one has never seen, but I shall be able to do things for the girls. Please make Papa understand that they cannot manage without Mallika coming in every day and make Faith able to look after Grace and Prudence.'

She was so concentrated on what she was saying that she did not realise for a second that her father had come to the end of one of his lengthy exhortations and was waiting for her response.

"*Amen*," she said quickly.

"The response should be, '*Good Lord, deliver us from evil*'," her father said in an irritated tone.

"I am sorry, Papa, *Good Lord, deliver us from evil.*"

"A*men.*"

The Vicar rose to his feet.

"We will pray a little longer when we are gathered together this evening, Dominica," he said. "I feel that our prayers will be like an armour to protect you from the difficulties and temptations that may lie ahead."

"Thank you, Papa."

Dominica went from the study leaving her father alone. She did not go back to the kitchen, instead she went up to her bedroom.

Over the mantelpiece there was a sketch of her mother. It had been roughly drawn by an amateur artist who had insisted on drawing Mrs. Radford soon after she was married.

He had actually excelled only in watercolour, but he had been an efficient enough draughtsman to put some of his subject's beauty down on paper and Dominica could fill in from memory all that he had left out.

Mrs. Radford had been a very pretty woman. She had the same blue eyes as Faith and her hair was fair, but Dominica had inherited her small straight nose and the soft curve of her lips.

The heart-shaped face was the same too and the winged eyebrows, which gave her a balanced look or what Lord Hawkston thought of as 'sensible'.

Dominica looked up at the picture.

"What would you have told me to do, Mama?" she asked aloud.

She waited almost expecting to hear an answer, but there was only the buzz of the bees as they sipped the honey from the climbing rose tree whose blossoms reached the windowsill of her bedroom.

"Suppose when we meet I hate him?" Dominica whispered. "Suppose he dislikes me?"

Then, as if she received an answer to her question, she told herself that she could return home.

She would go up to Kandy unmarried and, if Lord Hawkston was mistaken and she and his nephew took an immediate dislike to each other, then she was quite certain that he would realise that his proposal was insupportable and would pay her fare back to Colombo.

'In which case,' Dominica told herself practically, 'I have nothing to lose and if I should like him, then things could be very different.'

What was important was that she would be able to help the girls.

She knew that her father was growing more and more difficult to live with and he had in fact made things very hard for all of them since her mother's death.

For one thing he grudged every penny that was spent on food. Next month would be Lent and Dominica knew that he would try to insist on two fast-days a week.

Even out of Lent they regularly had one fast-day and the money saved was given to the poor of Colombo, many of whom, Dominica could not help thinking, ate a great deal better than they did.

Grace was always hungry and Prudence at all times had to be tempted to eat. Dominica was sure that it weakened her strength if she went for a whole day with nothing inside her but water.

Actually she cheated where the youngest was concerned.

"Why is Prudence having an egg?" Grace would enquire. "I thought that this was a day of abstinence."

"It's medicine where Prudence is concerned," was Dominica's invariable reply. "It would cost Papa a great deal more if we had to send for the doctor. I am sure she is anaemic."

"I am anaemic too."

"You are just greedy!" Faith interposed disparagingly.

"I don't see why we should have to go without food just to please Papa."

"It is not to please Papa, but to discipline ourselves like good Christians," Dominica would say automatically.

"Well, I would rather be a bad Christian and not feel so hungry," Faith said sharply. "Anyway there are some bananas in the garden and if there are half-a-dozen angels with flaming swords protecting them I still intend to eat one. It will at least stop my tummy rumbling."

Dominica often wondered what they would do without the garden where fruit grew wild and there were bananas, pawpaws, mangoes and many other fruits and vegetables indigenous to Ceylon.

Her father, of course, stuck strictly to his fast and always emerged from a day of abstinence a little harsher and, Dominica would think, more aggressive in his condemnation of evil and the sins of Society.

'When I am married,' she told herself now, 'the girls shall stay with me and I must find Faith a nice husband. The others shall lead an ordinary existence in a household where one need not have to pray over every crumb of bread and be eternally conscious of the sins of humanity.'

She felt guilty at such revolutionary thoughts, but she knew how impatient the older girls were with their father's fanatical asceticism and she knew that none of them had any real affection for him.

"I have tried to look after them as you did, Mama," she said, looking up again at her mother's picture, "but it has been difficult – very very difficult!"

She knew it would be worse for the others once she had left, but at the same time she would be able to ensure that sooner or later they could escape from the restrictions imposed on them by their father.

'What a pity,' she thought, 'that Lord Hawkston would not consider Faith as his nephew's wife. She would make a much more willing bride than I shall be.'

A bride!

It gave her a strange frightening feeling inside to think that she was to be the bride of a man she had never seen and had never heard of until an hour ago.

*

Lord Hawkston arrived the following morning before Dominica expected him.

She thought it very unlikely that he would appear before half past ten or eleven o'clock, but he must have let himself into the house because Dominica was down on her knees scrubbing the kitchen floor when he walked in.

She gave a startled exclamation as she saw his highly polished shoes advancing towards her. Then she sat back on her heels and looked up at him, the blood suddenly rising in her cheeks in her embarrassment.

"You were not expecting me?" Lord Hawkston asked in his deep voice.

"N-no, my Lord. It cannot be much after half past nine – and I thought that you would not be here until later."

"I am an early riser," Lord Hawkston said, "and we have a great deal to do, Dominica. I think the sooner we start the better."

"I will get ready, my Lord," Dominica said in a low voice.

She was very conscious of the large scrubbing brush in her hands, of the piece of coarse soap on the floor, the bucket of warm water beside her and the brown sacking apron she wore over her cotton dress.

She collected the soap and started to rise to her feet as Lord Hawkston asked,

"Do you have to do this?"

"Papa can only afford to pay – a woman to come in once a week," Dominica answered, "and the kitchen floor gets dirty very quickly."

"I can understand that," Lord Hawkston said gravely. "What will happen when you are no longer here?"

Dominica was now standing up, but before she replied she put the soap down on the edge of the table.

"I promised Faith, who hates domestic work, that I will try to persuade father to have Mallika, who is an excellent worker, every day once I have gone, but I am not certain that he will agree."

Dominica spoke in a worried voice and now she started to take off the rough apron, the bib of which reached nearly to her neck.

"I can see, Dominica," Lord Hawkston said, "that your leaving home will present a number of problems I had not anticipated. Would it make things any easier if I promise to pay Mallika's wages myself? After all I owe your father something for the inconvenience caused by taking away not only his daughter but apparently his 'maid-of-all-work'!"

He spoke a little quizzically. He knew that in no other house in Colombo would the lady of the house scrub her own floor.

The colour rose once again in Dominica's face.

"I think Papa might be too proud to allow you to pay the wages for what – ostensibly would be his own – servant," she said hesitatingly.

Then she added,

"No – that is not true. I think really that if you gave Papa the money for Mallika he would be sure to divert it to some family whom he considered to be more deserving than his own. In which case Faith would still have to clean the house or leave it dirty."

There was a faint smile on Lord Hawkston's lips as he said,

"I see I must find another solution. You shall pay Mallika with the money I give you for the purpose. Will that be more satisfactory?"

"It would indeed," Dominica replied with a little lilt in her voice. "But you are – sure you can – afford it?"

"Quite sure. As it happens, Dominica, I am what you would consider a rich man, so you need have no qualms about accepting from me not only the money for Mallika's wages but also for the trousseau we are now going to buy."

Dominica drew in her breath.

She seemed about to say something and then changed her mind.

"I will go and change," she said. "I would not wish to keep your Lordship waiting."

She left the kitchen before he could reply.

Lord Hawkston looked round him, noting the primitive stove, the bare floor, the hard chairs and the cheap china stacked on the dresser. Then he went from the kitchen into the sitting room where he had interviewed the Vicar and Dominica the previous day.

He had not to wait long.

He heard Dominica's footsteps hurrying down the uncarpeted stairway and she came into the room less than five minutes after leaving him.

She had changed into the dress that she had worn in Church, the same ugly black bonnet covered her hair and there were black cotton gloves on her hands.

"I am sorry I was not ready when you arrived, my Lord," she said in a tone as if she was still reproaching herself for being so tardy.

"Where are the rest of your family?" Lord Hawkston enquired.

"They are all with their teachers with the exception of Faith who has accompanied Papa because I was coming out with you. It meant that she could not have her French lesson."

She thought that Lord Hawkston looked faintly surprised and added by way of explanation,

"Mama insisted that however poor we were we should all have a good education. Sometimes Papa resents how much he has to pay and he wanted to stop Faith's lessons as soon as she reached the age of eighteen. But I persuaded him to let her continue for the rest of this year."

"You sound as if you missed your lessons," Lord Hawkston commented.

"More than I can ever say," Dominica answered. "It was like stepping into another world."

She gave a little sigh.

"If only I could get some more books!"

A thought struck her and there was a sudden light in her eyes as she asked,

"Will there be books at your plantation?"

"There were quite a number of them when I left, but what you cannot find on my bookshelves can easily be supplied. There is, I well know, a bookshop in Kandy and several in Colombo. You must tell me what your interests are, Dominica, I would like to hear about them."

As he spoke, he walked towards the front door, which was open, and she could see the carriage waiting outside.

Dominica could not help a little thrill of excitement as she stepped into the Governor's well-padded Victoria and the footman put a light rug over her knees.

Lord Hawkston seated himself beside her.

"What do you like reading?" he asked.

"Everything," Dominica replied, "but especially the histories of other countries and most especially about England."

"You have never been there?"

"No. Mama used to tell us what she did as a girl and of the Manor House where she lived in Gloucester. It all sounded fascinating."

"Do you like Ceylon?"

"Of course. It has always been my home and I love Colombo, the people, the flowers, and the sea. Mama always said that if we went to England we would miss the sunshine, but there would be many compensations."

"And what did she think those are?" Lord Hawkston asked in a slightly sceptical voice.

"I think Mama felt her roots were in England and that therefore the country – was a part of herself. I am sure that she was right and nationality is something far deeper and more fundamental than merely having a certain type of passport."

Lord Hawkston glanced at Dominica in surprise.

This was not the sort of remark he had expected from a young girl.

"So you want to travel?" he remarked.

"With my body, as I have travelled so much with my mind," Dominica replied. "But of course, my mind is the far cheaper method!"

She laughed as she spoke and Lord Hawkston noticed how it changed and illuminated her face.

They drove past the Racecourse on the sea front in silence and then Dominica enquired,

"Having lived for so long in Ceylon, where do you feel that you belong?"

"That is a question I have often asked myself," Lord Hawkston responded. "When I had to leave Ceylon two years ago, I felt that I was leaving everything that was familiar, everything I thought of as home. And yet, once back in England, I found so much that mattered to me because it was a part of my childhood, my adolescence and the time when I first thought of myself as a man."

"And so you loved it just as you loved Ceylon."

"I suppose that is true," Lord Hawkston agreed, but almost in surprise, as if he had not thought of it that way before.

They had now reached the more crowded streets teeming with every variety of Oriental race and costume.

There were the Ceylonese, the men as well as the women wearing their hair tied behind in knots, the women adding elaborate hairpins and there were the darker-skinned Tamils who came from India.

Hindus of every Caste jostled Moormen of Arab blood who introduced coffee to Ceylon, Afghan traders, Malay Policemen, long-nosed Parsees, narrow-eyed Chinese and there were Eurasians of Dutch or Portuguese or English descent.

It was all a kaleidoscope of movement, colour, noise and confusion.

"Where are you taking me?" Dominica asked.

"I have learnt from the Governor's most able and efficient Secretary," Lord Hawkston replied, "that the smartest and most important dressmaker in Ceylon is Madame Fernando."

Dominica turned to look at him with large eyes.

"So she is, but I must warn your Lordship that she is also very expensive."

"I have already assured you, Dominica, that you shall have the best and most beguiling trousseau that any girl could wish for. I therefore intend to introduce you to Madame Fernando, explain that the bills are to come to me, then leave you to choose what you and she think most suitable."

Dominica drew in her breath and turned her head to look straight in front of her.

Lord Hawkston was sure that she was thinking excitedly of what she would purchase.

What girl dressed as she was, in the cheapest material the marketplace could supply and made, he was quite certain by her own hands, could resist the lure of clothes which, if the Governor's Secretary was to be believed, were worn by all the smartest and most fashionable ladies in Colombo?

They reached Madame Fernando's shop, which displayed nothing in the window except an exceedingly smart bonnet trimmed with large ostrich plumes of crimson and blue.

It was obviously just decorative rather than anything that a lady would wish to wear, but Dominica looked at it with what Lord Hawkston thought were appreciative eyes and he wondered for the first time if he was wise to trust her taste.

Then, as the footman jumped down from the box of the carriage to open the door for them, Dominica turned impulsively.

"Please," she said to Lord Hawkston in a low voice, "will you choose what I should wear? I am sure that I will make mistakes and you will be ashamed of me."

Lord Hawkston was surprised.

He had planned exactly what he would do after he had left Dominica at the shop and where he would go before he returned to collect her.

He had never envisaged for a moment that he would be called upon to sit in a dressmaker's choosing gowns for a young woman, or to take an active part in providing her with a trousseau other than writing a cheque in payment for it.

Then with a faint smile on his lips he made up his mind.

"Why not?" he asked more to himself than to Dominica. "After all I have always believed that if one wants a thing done well, one should do it one's self. I will, as you suggest, stay with you, Dominica, but don't blame me if we have conflicting ideas as to how you should appear."

He saw the gratitude in her eyes and knew that she had not only been worried about making mistakes but felt shy at being in such a grand shop by herself.

Madame Fernando was, Lord Hawkston was prepared to admit, somewhat overpowering and he soon realised that, if he had not stayed with Dominica at her request, she would have had little say in the choosing of her trousseau.

French by birth, Madame Fernando had come to Colombo as the young bride of a Portuguese planter.

She had, however, soon grown tired of life on a plantation and had come to Colombo to procure orders for underclothes, which she embroidered skilfully for any lady who required them. She was fortunate in securing the patronage of the Governor's wife and from that moment her success was ensured.

At first she worked night and day to complete the orders she received and then she engaged the help of Ceylonese girls whom she taught to embroider as well as she could herself.

In ten years she was established as a dressmaker with a shop, a large staff and a Bank balance that increased year by year.

It was fortunate for her husband that the Bank balance was there when the coffee disease destroyed his plantation overnight.

Disgusted and disillusioned with Ceylon, he wished to return to Europe, but his wife however refused point blank to go with him.

She was happy in Colombo and she had also several attentive admirers she had no intention of leaving.

In the end Mr. Fernando went home without her. There was no question of a divorce as both of them were Catholics and Madame Fernando was quite certain that he would find plenty of charming ladies to console him in Lisbon.

Now Madame Fernando with shrewd eyes took in every detail of Lord Hawkston's appearance and she had already been informed by one of her receptionists in awestruck tones that he had arrived in the Governor's carriage.

"May I be of assistance, *monsieur*?" she asked in an ingratiating voice that had never lost its broken accent.

"I am Lord Hawkston and I need your help."

Madame Fernando dropped a curtsey.

"I am yours to command, my Lord."

"This young lady, Miss Dominica Radford, is to marry my nephew, Mr. Gerald Warren. She needs an entire trousseau."

There was a decided glitter of excitement in Madame Fernando's eyes as she replied,

"It will be a pleasure to dress anyone so charming as Mademoiselle."

She glanced, however, as she spoke at Dominica's gown and then looked away as if its material and shape made her shudder.

"There is one difficulty," Lord Hawkston explained.

Madame waited a little apprehensively.

"It is that we wish to leave not later than early on Thursday morning for Kandy, which means that Miss Radford must have enough gowns ready by then to travel in. The rest can be sent after her."

Madame Fernando drew in a deep breath of relief.

She had been half-expecting that Lord Hawkston was going to say that he could not afford to pay at once for all the things he desired. To hurry, however, would cost him more as the seamstresses would have to work late into the night to complete the orders.

But that was of little consequence.

"I have some dresses ready or half-finished that I am sure would suit Mademoiselle to perfection," Madame Fernando said. "May she put them on for your Lordship's approval?"

"We are in your hands, *madame*," his Lordship replied with an air that Madame Fernando could not help thinking was extremely attractive.

She said as much to Dominica as she took her to a dressing room, after she had given a dozen orders to the young Ceylonese girls to bring her what was required.

"My Lord, your uncle-in-law to be, *mademoiselle*, has an air *très distingué*. He is obviously, how you say in England, a great gentleman."

"He is very kind," Dominica answered, "but I would not wish to choose, *madame*, always the most expensive."

"Don't worry your head over such things," Madame Fernando said soothingly, "the cost is between Monsieur and myself. But first for you to show my gowns to perfection we must start with the right foundation."

She helped Dominica out of her dress and gave an exclamation of horror as she saw the plain calico underclothes beneath it.

For the first time in her life Dominica was laced into a corset, which gave her figure an elegance that she had not thought possible.

"You are thin, *mademoiselle*," Madame Fernando said. "That is good, but the shape must be right, a very small waist, the suspicion of a bosom and well-moulded hips."

She attended to Dominica as she spoke and when finally what she called the foundation of her gowns was achieved, Dominica could hardly believe that silk could feel so soft against her skin or that silk stockings could make such a difference to her legs.

Finally a gown was put over her head, which made her gasp with astonishment.

Of soft pink silk it seemed to accentuate the lights in her hair and the purity of her skin.

"It is too rich – too grand," Dominica protested, overawed by the frills and flounces, the small bustle and the little train that swept out behind her.

"I shall never have an occasion to wear anything so elaborate," she gasped.

"Let's show you to my Lord," Madame Fernando suggested. "There are a number of others for him to see if he does not like this one."

Dominica went out into the salon very shyly.

As she saw Lord Hawkston sitting at his ease in a damask-covered armchair, she felt that it had been audacious to ask him to stay with her and yet she doubted that she could have faced being left on her own.

Madame Fernando was to her mind terrifying and she was certain that Lord Hawkston would never have understood what gowns she had been compelled to buy unless he had actually been present at the transaction.

She awaited his verdict, her eyes on his face.

"Charming," he said at once. "It suits you, Dominica. Do you like it yourself?"

"I shall never have occasion – to wear such a gown," Dominica protested.

"I told you that my nephew was a gay young man. I am certain that he will want to take you into Kandy and you will find he has friends you will visit in the neighbourhood."

He turned towards Madame Fernando.

"That one must certainly be included in the trousseau, *madame*. What else have you for me to see?"

Dominica tried on six other gowns all of which Lord Hawkston insisted on buying and then a number of others were held up for his inspection, the majority of which he approved.

Finally Madame produced her *pièce de résistance*, a Wedding gown of white lace so beautiful and so alluring that when Dominica looked at herself in the mirror she could hardly believe that it was her own reflection.

There was a veil and a wreath of orange blossom.

"We shall have to alter your hairstyle, *mademoiselle*," Madame Fernando admonished her. "It's too severe, too harsh for a young lady of your age. I will send you a hairdresser. He will show you what is a more fashionable style."

"N-no, don't engage him until I am ready to receive him," Dominica said hastily.

She could not help thinking how horrified her father would be if he found a hairdresser in the Vicarage.

Equally she knew that Madame Fernando was speaking the truth in saying that the style that she did her hair in was not in keeping with the elegance of her new gowns.

To please Madame, who was very insistent, Dominica loosened the hair over her ears, made it fall from a parting in the middle in a soft wave on either side of her forehead and pinned it at the back into a chignon.

"That is better," Madame approved. "But you need curls on the top, *mademoiselle*, especially in the evening. They are very becoming."

"I will think – about it," Dominica faltered.

But somehow she felt that Lord Hawkston would agree with Madame Fernando.

She was well aware that he was not buying such delectable gowns entirely for her own satisfaction. She knew that he wished to make her look as attractive as the girl who had jilted his nephew and whom he therefore could not take with him to Kandy.

'I expect she is very pretty,' Dominica thought.

She wished that she could have seen the lady who had transferred her affections elsewhere as she would have some idea on what to model herself on.

Then she decided that to be a mere copy of another woman who had not honoured her word and had failed not only Gerald Warren but also his uncle would be a mistake.

For one thing it might annoy Lord Hawkston if he thought that she was equally frivolous and untrustworthy.

'I will be myself,' Dominica decided. 'I am Mama's daughter and Mama always said that we each of us have our own personalities, our own characters and our own standards. I will try to make the best of myself, but I will not try to imitate anyone else.'

The thought made her walk into the salon wearing the Wedding gown and made her appear as if she had stepped out of a Fairytale.

Lord Hawkston looked up at her for a long moment before he said quietly,

"It might have been designed for you."

"You approve, my Lord?" Madame Fernando enquired.

"I will take it with the rest of the gowns."

"Thank you, my Lord, thank you."

Madame Fernando turned away to give some instructions and Dominica moved nearer to Lord Hawkston.

"Are you sure that we should buy this gown?" she asked. "You don't think it – unlucky to anticipate that your nephew will accept me as his – wife?"

"I cannot think of any young man who would not eagerly accept you at this moment," Lord Hawkston replied. "Look in the mirror, Dominica. You will see for yourself how charming and attractive you look."

She gave him a faint smile, but at the same time her eyes were worried.

"You have done enough for one morning," he said. "Change into one of your new dresses and I will take you out to luncheon at the *Galle-face Hotel*."

Dominica looked surprised, but when she told Madame Fernando what was required she dressed her in a simple but exceedingly attractive gown of flowered muslin trimmed with pink ribbons.

There were new shoes to match the dresses and there were gloves and reticules to match most of them.

What was more to go with the gown that Dominica was wearing there was a little bonnet trimmed with a wreath of exquisite silk roses and ribbons of a soft pink to tie under her chin.

"Shall I throw away the clothes you arrived here in?" Madame Fernando enquired.

Dominica gave an exclamation of horror.

"No, of course not! There is a lot of wear in them still and I have five sisters younger than I am."

"Then you will no doubt have far more attractive clothes to hand down in future," Madame Fernando said with a smile.

"That is what I think myself," Dominica replied, "but in the meantime – "

Her voice died away.

She could not explain to Madame Fernando that her father would be horrified at the clothes she was wearing now and she was already worrying how, when she returned home, she could change quickly into one of her ordinary dresses before he saw her.

He had so often denounced as sinful the women in his congregation who dressed extravagantly. He was quite certain that frivolity was a sin and that beautiful clothes corrupted those who wore them.

"Please pack everything I came in," Dominica said, "and I will take them with me in the carriage."

"The gowns that are ready will be sent to the Vicarage this evening, *mademoiselle*," Madame Fernando told her. "The others will follow just as soon as they are finished until Thursday morning. After that the clothes will be sent by train to Kandy. I will speak about it with my Lord."

When Dominica came from the dressing room, it was to find Lord Hawkston writing a cheque.

She knew that it must be for an enormous sum and she felt exceedingly guilty that so much money had been spent on clothes that could have fed those who were hungry.

But it was impossible not to be thrilled with her appearance and the fact that she possessed so many delectable things, so many she could hardly remember how many there relly were.

She reached Lord Hawkston's side as he was handing the cheque to Madame Fernando and he turned to smile at her.

Her eyes were on his face and he saw that there was a pleading expression in them.

"What is it?" he asked.

"I want to ask you – something," Dominica said. "You may refuse, but I must – ask you."

"Tell me," he said quietly.

She drew him a little to one side out of earshot of Madame.

"It is just that you have given me so much, so much more than I expected or even dreamt of. Could we possibly give back one dress and buy new bonnets for my sisters? We have worn the black ones ever since Mama died and they will have to go on wearing them for years and years! We all hate black!"

There was a little throb in her voice and her eyes pleaded with him to understand.

"Just one dress less?" Dominica pleaded. "It would cost you no more."

Lord Hawkston smiled at her and then turned towards Madame Fernando.

"Madame," he said. "I have another commission for you."

"But, of course, my Lord," she smiled.

"There are," Lord Hawkston said slowly, "five more Miss Radfords of varying ages. I would like you to make a simple Sunday dress such as Miss Dominica is wearing now for each of them. They will also require bonnets to match, each one to be different and suitable to their particular age and individuality. I think it would be wisest if you send someone to the Vicarage, perhaps this evening, to measure them."

"It will be a pleasure, my Lord," Madame Fernando said in a gratified voice.

She bowed Lord Hawkston and Dominica out of the shop with many expressions of gratitude.

When finally they drove away in the carriage, Dominica turned towards Lord Hawkston.

"I did not know anyone could be so marvellously and wonderfully kind!" she exclaimed. "Thank you, my Lord. Thank you with all my heart."

"It has been a pleasure, Dominica," he replied and meant it.

CHAPTER FOUR

The train was moving at what seemed to Dominica to be great speed through a succession of rice fields and swamps.

She sat looking out, feeling as she had felt from the moment Lord Hawkston came into her life that everything was happening in a dream and that there was no reality or substance about it.

Up to the very last moment she could hardly believe that she was really leaving the Vicarage for good and saying 'goodbye' to her sisters.

They had been almost too excited about the new dresses and bonnets Lord Hawkston was giving them from Madame Fernando's to be upset at the thought of Dominica leaving them.

When she first told them what he had ordered, they could hardly believe it was true.

"Will Papa let us wear them?" Faith asked at last. "What will he say when he sees us in such grand clothes?"

"He will say," Charity remarked, mimicking her father's voice, "'a woman's conceit and her lust for rich attire is an abomination in the eyes of the Lord'!"

"I am quite certain that he will make us go on wearing our old dresses and those hateful hideous bonnets!" Faith declared despairingly.

"I thought about that coming home," Dominica said. "Although perhaps it is wrong of me, I can tell you what you must do."

"What is that?" the older girls asked in unison.

"When your new bonnets arrive, burn your old ones!"

"*Burn* them?"

The words were almost a shriek.

"You know as well as I do," Dominica went on, "that Papa would never let you spend money on buying a new bonnet if you had one that was still wearable. And you could not go to Church bareheaded."

Faith put her arms around Dominica and hugged her.

"You are a genius," she exclaimed. "That is exactly what we will do."

"Perhaps it is a little deceitful," Dominica said hesitatingly, "but I am sure that the gowns will be lovely – as lovely as mine – and Lord Hawkston told Madame Fernando that they were all to be different."

"He is the most wonderful man in the world!" Faith cried exultantly.

"Be careful not to thank him in front of Papa," Dominica admonished her.

They remembered her warning although it was difficult to say nothing until the moment came when they were alone with him.

Then their gratitude burst forth.

"How can you be so kind?"

"It's so exciting!"

"We can hardly believe that you are giving us such wonderful presents."

"I shall look forward to seeing you dressed as you should be," Lord Hawkston smiled and Dominica fancied that there was a twinkle in his eyes.

Prudence, who had said little, now came to stand beside him.

"I think you're very kind," she said with a slight lisp. "I'll marry you when I am grown up!"

Lord Hawkston looked somewhat startled, but he said,

"I am very honoured at receiving the first proposal of marriage any lady has ever made to me!"

"You'll wait for me?" Prudence enquired.

He looked down at her and realised that she was a small replica of Dominica. She had the same ash-blonde hair, grey eyes and small straight nose.

She looked fragile and he guessed that she was the weakest member of the family.

"Will you wait?" Prudence asked again earnestly.

"I'll tell you what I will promise you," Lord Hawkston said after a moment's pause. "When you are eighteen, I will give a grand ball at which you shall meet all the most handsome, eligible and charming young men of my acquaintance."

Prudence's eyes lit up.

"I must learn to dance."

"You must also be strong and eat up all your food," Dominica interposed, "otherwise you will not be strong enough to dance all night. Is that not true, my Lord?"

She glanced at Lord Hawkston meaningfully as she spoke.

"It is indeed," he said gravely. "Dancing can be very strenuous. It would be extremely disappointing if, like Cinderella, you had to leave your own ball at twelve o'clock."

"I'll eat," Prudence promised.

It was clever of him, Dominica thought now as she looked out of the train, to give the child an inducement. There had been so many struggles in the past because Prudence was fastidious and found the very limited fare that their father would permit unpalatable.

The rice fields alternated with jungle-covered knolls that seemed like small islands surrounded by the emerald green of the young rice. Dominica could see the splay-footed buffalo hitched on to wooden ploughs floundering up to their knees where the wet ground was being prepared for a new crop.

From Rambukana it was a steady climb and another engine was hitched to the first.

At one point, which Dominica knew was called 'Sensation Rock', the line was cut into the steep side of the mountain and the view was fantastic.

There was a precipice of seven hundred feet below them and below that another descent of more than one thousand feet to the paddy fields.

The hills near the railway were covered with young tea plants growing between the stumps of dead coffee trees, but most of the time they were passing through forest.

Lord Hawkston sat opposite Dominica, but feeling that he would not wish to talk above the noise of the engine, she looked out at the scenery deep in her own thoughts.

She was conscious that her travelling dress was very elegant and the small jacket that lay beside her on another seat was beautifully cut.

When her sisters had seen her wearing her new bonnet trimmed with flowers, they were awestruck into silence until Faith, breaking the tension, asked,

"How many years will you have to wear that gown before I can have it?"

"I will send it to you as soon as I am given another," Dominica promised her.

There were so many things to do at the last moment and so many instructions to give to Mallika that Dominica had little time to think about her own feelings or to worry about what lay ahead.

Only in the darkness of the night had she felt a little tremor of fear when she thought of Gerald Warren waiting for her and wondered if he was feeling as apprehensive about her as she was about him.

She at least could picture him as being very like his uncle and that was a consolation in itself.

But he had no yardstick to measure her by and she wondered if perhaps he was feeling angry and rebellious at the idea of being married off to a stranger.

She knew that Lord Hawkston had written to his nephew on Monday and to make quite certain that he received the letter and that it was not delayed he had sent it by a bearer, paying the fare of the man from Colombo to the plantation and back again.

Lord Hawkston did not tell Dominica whether he had told the bearer to wait for an answer. She fancied that he had not expected one, being quite certain that his nephew would obey his wishes without argument.

All the same it was impossible not to feel extremely apprehensive as the train, after a four hour journey, steamed into Kandy and Dominica was told that they were to change trains for the last part of their journey.

She had always been told that Kandy was beautiful and that it was the last stronghold of the Ceylonese Kings with its Sacred Temple of the Tooth overlooking an artificial lake.

But she had not expected it to be quite so glorious.

There were over two hours to wait before their connecting train went on into the Central Province, which would take them, Lord Hawkston said, within five miles of his plantation.

Because he knew it would interest her he hired a carriage and they drove through the town and along the side of the lake.

Everywhere there were orchids, jasmines, magnolias, the orange and crimson flowers of the asocas and the delicate white blossoms of the champee, which had a strong and lovely scent.

"Did you know that Krishna, the Hindu God of Love, tips his arrows with the champee flowers?" Dominica asked.

"Does that make them more effective?" Lord Hawkston enquired with a smile.

"The Brahmins think so."

Then daringly she asked,

"Have you ever been in love, my Lord?"

"Not enough to wish to sacrifice my freedom," he replied.

"That means your answer is 'no'," Dominica said. "I am sure if one is really in love there is no sacrifice one would not make and nothing one would not relinquish"

"You sound as if you have been reading some very romantic novels," he said accusingly.

"Papa would not allow a novel in the house, but I know love – real love – if we find it, would be too strong for us to – resist it."

Even as she spoke she knew that she was being indiscreet to talk in such a manner with Lord Hawkston, seeing that he had persuaded her to marry his nephew without love and without even affection.

But the beauty all around her made her almost irresistibly think of love.

As if he wished to change the subject, Lord Hawkston told Dominica how brave the Kandyans had been and how they were the last inhabitants of Ceylon to hold out against the conquest of the country by the British.

He told her too about Asia's most spectacular pageant, the *Esala Perahera*, which had been held at Kandy for at least the last two thousand years.

"You will enjoy it," he said. "The gaily caparisoned elephants, the drummers and dancers, the Chieftains in jewelled costumes and the whip-crackers all combine to make it the most impressive spectacle I have ever seen."

"I have often wondered how or why Ceylon possessed the tooth of Buddha," Dominica remarked.

As she spoke, she was watching the women in their brilliant saris climbing the steps into the Temple. In their hands they carried the flowers of the champee tree to lie like prayers before the shrine.

"The famous relic is said by legend to have come here concealed in the hair of a Princess fleeing from India during a war," Lord Hawkston replied.

He paused to add with a smile,

"I suspect her hair was as long and luxuriant as yours."

Dominica blushed.

"How do you know – my hair is – like that?"

"I guessed that you have difficulty in arranging it."

Dominica looked worried.

"Perhaps I could be more fashionable if I cut some of it off."

"You are to do nothing of the kind," Lord Hawkston stipulated positively. "A woman should have long hair, it is part of her femininity, and undoubtedly yours is your crowning glory."

Dominica blushed again, at the same time she felt a little glow of delight at his words. They were a compliment!

There were so many things she wanted to ask him and so much she wanted to learn that all too quickly it was time to return to the Station and once again they were travelling Northward.

"This is very different," he said as the train moved out of the Station, "from the days when I first bought my plantation, when I used to have to ride down to Kandy. There was only a dusty track for us to convey the coffee by bullock cart."

He smiled and added,

"Now we can hardly visualise the days when Governor North made a tour of the island with one hundred and sixty palanquin bearers, four hundred coolies, two elephants and fifty lascoreens!"

"It must have given them many a headache to try to accommodate such a large party," Dominica exclaimed.

She tried to talk naturally, but every mile they progressed made her feel more nervous and more afraid.

She knew only too well that Lord Hawkston expected her to be calm and sensible. That after all was the reason why he had chosen her to be the wife of his nephew and if she appeared at all hysterical he would despise her.

Accordingly she forced herself to speak naturally and she was aware that he was trying to put her at her ease and make everything seem quite commonplace.

"I told Gerald in my letter not after all to meet us at Kandy," he said. "I thought it would be difficult for you to converse together for the first time in a rattling train. You will meet him at the house I built myself and I am very proud of it."

"Was it a difficult task?" Dominica asked.

"It was one I greatly enjoyed," Lord Hawkston replied. "At first the building was much smaller than it is now and my plans received a setback when the coffee failed. Then, when tea began to come into its own, I resumed the work and the house and garden were actually completed only a year before I had to return to England."

There was a note in his voice that told Dominica all too clearly that this was another reason why he hated to leave Ceylon.

"Perhaps as a woman you will find many things that I have omitted," he said with a smile, "but to me my house seemed nearly perfect and its position could not be improved on anywhere else in Ceylon."

"I am sure that I shall admire it very much," Dominica said in a low voice.

She hoped as she spoke that she would also admire its present occupant.

Supposing Gerald Warren had a broken heart for the girl he had lost and could not bear the thought of another woman taking her place?

'I must be very kind and understanding,' Dominica told herself.

She was used to being gentle and compassionate.

After her mother had died her father often insisted that she went with him when he visited the families in the native quarters whom he considered his special charges.

Many of them were old, ill or dying. Some of them were deformed. A number of children were sick.

As if he read her thoughts. Lord Hawkston asked unexpectedly,

"What did you do when you accompanied your father on his visiting?"

"Papa is always trying to convert the Ceylonese to Christianity," Dominica answered. "Mama used to say he should have been a Missionary. There are many families who have been baptised by Papa and he never allows them to become indifferent to their promises."

She gave a little smile.

"Sometimes I think he bullies them into being Christians whether they like it or not. He is certainly very severe if they miss Church on Sunday without a really valid excuse."

Lord Hawkston was quite certain that the Ceylonese, who were an easy-going and friendly people, were easily pressured by the Vicar into doing what he wished, but aloud he said,

"You have not told me what you did."

"I looked after the children while Papa remonstrated with their parents or I would try to make the elderly and the sick comfortable. I think many of them just enjoyed seeing me because I was someone to talk to."

"I can believe that," Lord Hawkston commented.

Dominica looked out of the train.

Walking along the roadway that ran beside the railway line she could see a Buddhist Priest in the bright saffron yellow robe that proclaimed his calling.

"I can never understand," she said speaking her thoughts aloud, "why any Buddhist should ever be willing to change his religion to Christianity. Buddhism is such a happy religion."

"You have read about it?" Lord Hawkston enquired.

"And talked with many Buddhists," Dominica replied and then added hastily, "Not that Papa would have approved, but I was so interested in their beliefs, in fact I have often wished that I was a Buddhist."

"Perhaps you were in a previous incarnation," Lord Hawkston suggested.

She smiled at him.

"Do you, like them, believe in reincarnation?"

"Shall I say I consider it a possibility," he replied.

Dominica's eyes were alight with interest.

"It seems the only just – the only right explanation of all the troubles and ills of the world," she said. "The Priests are so dedicated, yet quiet and unobtrusive. They never force their convictions on anyone."

Lord Hawkston knew that she was thinking of what a contrast they were to her father.

He had begun in the last few days to realise that Dominica was extremely intelligent and thought far more seriously than he would have expected any other girl of her age to do.

He supposed in a way it was part of her unusual upbringing and yet despite her ignorance of the social world he could not help realising that she had a mind that could not be confined and would touch heights that other people would never reach.

"I will tell you something that will please you," he said unexpectedly.

"What is that?" Dominica enquired.

"I have already written to the bookshop in Kandy to despatch a consignment of their very latest volumes to the plantation."

The way Dominica's face lit up told him how pleased she was even before the words came to her lips.

"You will have plenty of time for reading," Lord Hawkston said, "when Gerald is out in the fields, but there is one thing I must say to you."

"What is that?" Dominica asked a little nervously.

"You must not do any work in the house yourself."

"Why not?" she queried.

"Because you will have an adequate supply of servants and to take over what is their work would be to insult them and suggest that you do not think they are competent."

"And if they do things wrong?"

"Then, of course, you can explain exactly what you require," Lord Hawkston replied. "But no scrubbing, no washing or dusting!"

"What about cooking?" Dominica asked faintly.

"The cook I have in my house is extremely proficient. If by any chance he has left, which I think is highly unlikely, then of course you can teach whoever takes his place, but you are not, and let me make this quite clear, Dominica, you are not to cook yourself."

She gave a little sigh and then she said,

"I can see you are turning me into a grand lady. No wonder you have ordered a number of books for me to read. But what *may* I do?"

"You can ride for one thing," Lord Hawkston answered "I have a feeling that you would look well on a horse."

"We used to ride a pony when we were children," Dominica said, "but when he died we could not afford another one."

"I will teach you to ride," Lord Hawkston said and then added as if it was an afterthought, "unless Gerald wishes to do so himself."

The train drew up at the Station where they were to disembark at about half past three in the afternoon.

Before they reached Kandy they had eaten at midday out of a delicious luncheon basket that Lord Hawkston had brought with him from the Queen's House.

There had been delectable and exciting dishes such as Dominica had never tasted before and there was a golden wine to drink, which she felt was bottled sunshine.

Now, as they stepped out of the Station, she felt a little sick and wondered if it was from an inner fear or whether she had eaten too much at luncheon.

There was a carriage waiting for them and, as Lord Hawkston directed the porter who was collecting the luggage from the van, a Ceylonese man came towards him.

"Ranjan!" Lord Hawkston exclaimed. "How nice of you to meet me."

He shook the man by the hand then turned to Dominica,

"This is Ranjan, Dominica," he said, "my Overseer, whom I left in charge when I went to England. It is good to see you, Ranjan."

"You too, *Durai*," Ranjan replied. "We are hoping you come back."

"Is everything all right?" Lord Hawkston asked.

"No, *Durai*, Plenty trouble," Ranjan replied.

"I heard that there were some difficulties," Lord Hawkston said, "but it is something, I promise you, I will put right."

"What happen now no one put right," Ranjan said in a low voice.

Tactfully Dominica turned aside, but she could still hear what the two men were saying.

"What has happened?" Lord Hawkston asked sharply.

"Seetha, girl *Sinna Durai* turn away, dead. We find body bottom of torrent this morning."

Dominica was aware that Lord Hawkston was suddenly rigid. He had stopped moving and was standing in the sunshine facing the Overseer whose sarong was a patch of colour against the wooden walls of the Station buildings.

"She killed herself," Lord Hawkston said almost beneath his breath.

"Yes, *Durai*. Lakshman, Seetha's father, swear revenge!"

"You must find him, Ranjan," Lord Hawkston said firmly. "Find him immediately. Tell him how I will give him full compensation and more for what he has suffered."

"I try, *Durai*," Ranjan answered, "but he plenty mad. Too late for money."

"You must try, Ranjan. Say I have just arrived. Say I am extremely upset at what has occurred and ask him to come and see me immediately."

"I do that, *Durai*," Ranjan answered, but Dominica thought that his tone was doubtful.

"I will see you later," Lord Hawkston said.

Then in another tone of voice to Dominica,

"Come, Dominica, you should not stand in the sunshine without your sunshade to protect you."

"No, of course not," Dominica replied.

Obediently she opened her sunshade and held it over her head.

Some of the luggage was piled onto the carriage they were to travel in, the rest Ranjan took with him in a rather curiously shaped cart, made of halmila wood, which Dominica guessed was used for carrying vegetables or bamboo about the plantation.

The carriage that drew Lord Hawkston and Dominica set off at a good pace, but once they had left the station the way was uphill and they soon slowed down.

Lord Hawkston did not speak and after a moment Dominica asked a little nervously,

"Who is – Seetha?"

"You heard what my Head man said to me?"

"I could not help it."

"He should have been more discreet," Lord Hawkston said sharply.

"You said the girl had – killed herself. Why?"

She knew that her question was unwelcome and yet some instinct told her that what had been said was of importance to her.

After a distinct pause Lord Hawkston answered,

"You have lived in Ceylon all your life, Dominica, and you must have been aware what a lonely isolated life the average planter lives in the hills. He is alone with only his coolies. That is why I was so anxious to find a suitable wife for my nephew."

"Seetha is Ceylonese," Dominica said, her eyes on Lord Hawkston's face.

"Her name makes it obvious," he said abruptly. "She must have been mentally deranged to throw herself down the torrent. It is a drop of hundreds of feet and if she fell on the rocks she would be rendered unconscious and therefore would be easily drowned by the falling water."

"Why did she kill herself?" Dominica persisted.

Lord Hawkston did not answer and after a moment she said in a very small voice,

"Was it – anything to do with– Mr. Warren turning her away? That is whom your Overseer meant by *Sinna Durai*, was it not?"

Lord Hawkston had contemplated lying and then he knew that it would be an insult to Dominica's intelligence.

It was unfortunate that Ranjan had blurted out in front of her the news of Seetha's death, but he was not to know that Lord Hawkston had a wife for the *Sinna Durai* with him.

Ranjan in fact, as Lord Hawkston was well aware, was so worried and distraught by what had occurred that it had never entered his mind to be discreet in front of a stranger.

Choosing his words carefully Lord Hawkston said slowly,

"There are always women, Dominica, who are ready to supply the female companionship that young planters find essential when they are always alone."

Although she made no movement, he felt that Dominica winced. He had the feeling that she had half-expected it and yet it was a shock when it was put into words.

"You mean – that Mr. Warren and Seetha were in – love with each other?" she asked in a hesitating voice.

"I mean nothing of the sort," Lord Hawkston replied. "It is not a question of love as you and I think of it, Dominica. It is just that a man has a physical need for a woman and when a woman is ready to supply that need it can become an amicable businesslike arrangement."

Dominica was silent for some moments.

Then at length she said,

"I think this must be one of the – temptations that Papa preaches against so fervently. He tried to have the places closed in Colombo where the planters met Ceylonese women because he thought such – associations were – wicked."

"Your father has, understandably, rather extreme views on the matter," Lord Hawkston said coldly. "But after all, until your mother died he was a married man, and therefore not subject to loneliness or to the temptations which, may I say quite frankly, are recognised by most people in this part of the world."

"The girl killed – herself," Dominica said. "Why did your nephew – send her away?"

"Let me tell you at once," Lord Hawkston answered, "that this is nothing to do with your coming here and the letter I sent to my nephew announcing our arrival. It actually happened before I had even arrived back in Colombo."

He felt that his explanation might make things better. But he saw that Dominica was very pale and there was an expression in her grey eyes that he could not fathom.

That she was shocked at what had occurred was predictable, but he could only hope that, if she understood that the situation had nothing to do with her personally, it would not disturb her unduly.

They drove in silence for a little while and then Lord Hawkston said,

"I want you to promise me something, Dominica,"

"What is it?" she asked in a low voice.

"You and I have become friends these last few days and I like to think that you trust my judgement, Will you trust me a little further when I tell you to forget what you overheard just now and put the whole incident out of your mind? Leave me to arrange matters as I think best."

There was a little pause before Dominica said,

"I will – try."

"You must remember that we have only heard one side of the story," Lord Hawkston added. "I was told when I first arrived in Colombo that there was some difficulty over this woman, but I have not yet heard what Gerald has to say about it. I know you will agree that we must be fair and hear his explanation before we blame him in any way for what may just have been an unfortunate accident."

Dominica could not answer and Lord Hawkston went on,

"As you can imagine, the coolies on the plantation who have little to think about exaggerate everything dramatically. They make a drama out of every small occurrence. I am confident that when I get to the bottom of things I will find it quite different from what we at present suspect."

As he spoke, Lord Hawkston only wished that he could feel as optimistic as he sounded.

James Taylor had told him that Gerald was making a mess of things, but it was now very much worse than when James had come to see him in Colombo and warn him of what he might expect.

'Damn the young fool,' Lord Hawkston thought to himself and he was well aware that what had happened would travel like lightning round the neighbourhood.

What was more it would unsettle the work-people and do harm to the plantation. That, he thought, he could never forgive.

He himself had the reputation of being a hard taskmaster, but a completely just one.

He had also paid his workers generously. Despite the fact that he worked them hard, his coolies had all respected and had been loyal to him.

He could never remember a man leaving because he thought that he would find a better job elsewhere or being disgruntled at the treatment he received.

What could Gerald have been doing during the past two years? And how could he have destroyed the goodwill and confidence of an estimable man like Ranjan?

The only redeeming feature, Lord Hawkston told himself, was that neither Seetha nor her father was employed on the plantation.

That would have been the worst mistake of all and he could only be thankful that Gerald had not committed the unforgivable mistake of tampering with one of his own employees.

If Lakshman, Seetha's father, would not come to see him, Lord Hawkston decided that he must seek him out.

He had an idea that he belonged to a small village in the hills that was not far from the house.

'It will be a question of money,' he said to himself and hoped that it would prove to be so.

The Ceylonese were a quiet gentle people, but what worried Lord Hawkston was that Lakshman might in his grief and anger have gone mad. He had known it happen before and the consequences could be very unpleasant.

In the meantime he had two problems, to find Lakshman and to allay Dominica's anxiety.

Lord Hawkston was not insensitive.

He knew that to any girl, especially one with as much character and personality as Dominica, it would be a shock to learn that the man she was about to marry had not only had a mistress but had also driven her to her death.

Too late he realised that the moment Ranjan began to speak of trouble he should have guessed it concerned Gerald and should have taken him out of earshot.

But he had supposed that the man was referring to something that had happened to the crops. It was always prevalent in his mind because of the coffee disaster.

Even now he would sometimes wake in the night to find himself sweating with horror as he recalled how he had put out his hands to pluck the leaves and rubbing the diseased patches, trying to tell himself that it was not the fungoid that he suspected, and yet even as he did so knowing that there was no hope.

It was with a tremendous effort that Lord Hawkston managed to speak lightly and, he hoped, normally as he said aloud,

"When we round the next turn of the road, you will see my house,"

They had been climbing all the time and the air, though still warm, had a freshness about it that Dominica had not known in Kandy.

As they reached the corner, Lord Hawkston said,

"Close your eyes!"

Dominica obeyed him and then heard him order the carriage to draw to a standstill. There was a moment's pause before he said,

"Look now!"

Below them was a deep valley surrounded by hills and behind them again there was a range of high-peaking green mountains. Directly ahead of them there was a cascade pouring downwards into a lake and descending again hundreds of feet in a torrent of silver.

Almost blinding in the sunshine Dominica could see beside it a long, low white house with wide verandahs on two floors.

The gardens surrounding it were a mosaic of colour, a blaze of jungle flame, yellow, gold, white-pink, purple and even blue, which she knew belonged to the nelu, which could carpet the ground with its rare blooms.

Below the house, rising from the depths of the valley to the edge of the garden, were the dark green tea plants luxuriantly filling their terraces, which were like steps rising towards a Temple.

Dominica drew in her breath.

She knew Lord Hawkston was waiting for her to speak and at last she said,

"Now I know why Adam and Eve came to Ceylon!"

"You think this is another Eden?"

"The original could not have been more exquisitely breathtakingly beautiful!"

She knew that he was pleased not merely at her words but by her sincerity.

"That was what I thought," he said quietly, "when I first saw the valley."

The view was so lovely and in a way so unexpected that Dominica sat staring at it spellbound.

"Do you like the house I built?" Lord Hawkston asked.

"It is lovely, very lovely!"

"Do you really think so?"

"It looks like something from a Fairytale," she answered. "I feel sure that the lake is enchanted."

"You must learn to swim."

"I have always wanted to, but Papa would not let us go – into the sea. He said it was immodest."

"No one will see you here," Lord Hawkston assured her, "especially if you bathe when everyone else is at work."

"I will do so."

Then he saw Dominica glance at the torrent below the lake and he knew that she was remembering that Seetha had met her death by throwing herself down it.

His lips tightened in a hard line and he knew that whatever he might say, however hard he might try to prevent it, the tragedy of Seetha's death would overshadow Dominica's arrival.

He signalled to the coachman and the carriage began to move more swiftly as the road went straight along the side of the hill towards the house.

It was the road he had built himself and he thought that it was a considerable achievement that he could well be proud of.

The house drew nearer and as it did so he felt that Dominica was pressing herself back against the cushions of the carriage as if in sudden weakness.

He smiled at her.

"Don't be nervous," he advised. "There are so many interesting things to see and so much I want to show you that I know you are going to enjoy yourself."

Dominica turned to look at him and he saw the anxiety in her eyes.

"It's all right," he said quietly. "Just trust me as I have asked you to do."

"I will – try," she murmured.

*

It was not until Dominica had gone to bed that Lord Hawkston had a chance to speak to his nephew.

Gerald Warren had met them in the hall as the carriage drew up at the front door of the house and, as he had stepped forward with what his uncle thought was a somewhat forced smile on his face, Lord Hawkston received his second shock of the day.

In two years Gerald Warren had altered almost out of all recognition.

He had put on at least three stone in weight, his face was red and puffy and even before he smelt the spirit on his breath Lord Hawkston knew the cause of such a change.

When he had last seen him, Gerald had been slim, smart and had an undoubted charm that made women like Emily Ludgrove find him easy to love.

Life in Ceylon had swept away his elegance and changed him to a point where his uncle could hardly believe that he was the same person.

He had obviously been drinking before they arrived, although he was, Lord Hawkston noticed, formally attired and had made himself as presentable as possible.

He was quite obviously on edge at meeting both his uncle and Dominica, but, as the evening progressed and he had consumed a considerable amount of whisky, he grew more relaxed.

His raucous laugh rang out, interspersed with long grumbles about the difficulties of tea planting and the boredom of being so far from civilisation.

Lord Hawkston had been sure that Gerald would make an effort, but if this was the best he could do it was not very impressive.

He hoped, however, that Dominica, not having known him before, would not be as surprised at his appearance as he was and would find him, because he was young and near her age, at least pleasant.

He himself found as the hours passed a cold fury growing inside him at the idea that any young man could have failed so completely in a position of trust and had not even appreciated the opportunity that he had been offered.

'It's my fault. I should never have sent him here,' Lord Hawkston told himself.

But the fact that he had been in the wrong did not make him any less angry.

He managed, during dinner, to keep the conversation at least tolerably interesting and he only hoped that Dominica was not aware of the amount of whisky, or its strength, that Gerald was consuming.

He thought that she was tired and she confirmed this when she rose to her feet soon after they had finished coffee in the sitting room whose long high windows overlooked the valley.

"I think, if you will excuse me, my Lord., I will retire," she said to Lord Hawkston. "It has been a long day."

"It has indeed," he replied. "Goodnight, Dominica, and I hope you sleep well."

"I am sure I shall," Dominica replied. "Goodnight, my Lord. Goodnight, Mr. Warren."

She curtseyed to both gentlemen and went from the room.

Lord Hawkston had already been annoyed on arrival to find that Gerald had shut up the top of the house where he had always slept and they were all using the bedrooms on the ground floor.

"Why have you done this?" he enquired.

"I could not afford so many servants," his nephew replied with a truculent note in his voice. "There was no point in having them sitting about doing nothing."

Because Dominica was there Lord Hawkston checked the words that came to his lips.

He was well aware that on the generous allowance he had made to Gerald before he left for England he could have afforded as many servants as were necessary.

He guessed from what James Taylor had told him that Gerald's allowance had been frittered away on riotous living and whisky.

He was careful, however, not to show his anger until the door closed behind Dominica and he was alone with his nephew.

It was then that he spoke in a controlled quiet voice, but with every word as effective as a whiplash.

"I have heard about Seetha's death," he began. "How could you have been such a fool, such a *damned* fool, as to dismiss her without the usual payment? Anyone round here could have told you how much she was entitled to."

"I was well aware of how much she expected," Gerald said surlily, "but I hadn't got it. Do you understand? I had not got the money!"

"You could have at least promised that you would give it to her on my arrival," Lord Hawkston said, "or the Bank would have advanced you a loan."

"I have already had a loan."

"How much?"

"A thousand pounds and they would not give me any more."

"You have spent a thousand pounds over and above what I sent you?" Lord Hawkston asked incredulously.

"There are also some debts," his nephew said defiantly.

Lord Hawkston walked across the room trying to control his temper.

"I see now that you were too stupid and too idle to take on a job of this sort," he said. "But I believed in you and thought that you had the qualities required to carry on my work here. I was mistaken."

"I would like to go back to England."

"And when you go there what do you intend to do? Live on your mother? She has very little money, as you well know, and you have spent most of it already."

"At least I shall be with civilised people."

"Now listen, Gerald," Lord Hawkston asserted. "I am not going to permit you to behave like a spoilt child and go running back to your mother just because you have made a mess of everything here."

His tone sharpened as he continued,

"It is unfortunate that Emily Ludgrove changed her mind about marrying you, but I think if you had come to Colombo to see her she would have been so shocked by your appearance that she would have broken off the engagement anyway."

"I never really thought Emily would marry me," Gerald Warren said, "not if she had known that she had to live in this dead-and-alive hole."

"Well, this is where you are going to live," Lord Hawkston announced angrily. "I have brought you a wife who will look after you and, I hope, keep you in order. I will get the plantation back into working order and then when I return to England you will carry on until I can find someone more adequate to take your place. Is that clear?"

"What is the alternative?" Gerald enquired.

"The alternative," Lord Hawkston said slowly and his voice was harsh, "is that you work your passage home Steerage. You will never have another penny piece of my money and I shall make sure on my return to England that you have none of your mother's."

There was a silence and then Gerald Warren threw back his head and laughed. It was an ugly jeering sound.

"You've got it all nicely tied up, haven't you, Uncle Chilton? You have me in chains and there is nothing I can do about it. Very well. I'll marry the wife you have chosen for me. She's quite a pretty little thing and perhaps she will contrive to make this place seem less like a mausoleum. I imagine you will give us enough to live on?"

"I will pay your debts," Lord Hawkston said, "and I will give you an allowance that in Ceylon will make you seem comparatively rich as long as you stop drinking."

"Entirely?"

"You will sign the pledge!"

"Now really, uncle – " Gerald began in a conciliatory tone.

"Those are my conditions," Lord Hawkston interrupted. "Take them or leave them."

There was a pause.

"Very well, blast it, I'll take them!" Gerald exclaimed.

He stared at his uncle with undeniable animosity in his eyes and then he picked up the whisky bottle.

"If I have to sign the pledge tomorrow," he said, "I might as well enjoy myself tonight. Thank you. Uncle Chilton, for your generosity. I am sure you expect me to be deeply and humbly grateful."

His voice was sarcastic.

It would have been a more dignified exit had he not staggered against the side of the door as he left the room.

CHAPTER FIVE

Dominica lay awake thinking over what had happened during the day.

She had been tired when she came to bed, but she had been unable to sleep.

She found herself shrinking from the thought of Gerald Warren and, while she knew in her heart that she could never marry him, she dared not express such a decision in words.

The difficulty would be how to explain it to Lord Hawkston.

She had quite confidently believed that Gerald would look very like his uncle and she had repeated to herself over and over again Lord Hawkston's description of him as tall and good-looking.

When she had seen the fat red-faced man waiting for them in the hall, she had not at first realised that this was in fact the man she had come to meet, the man she had promised to marry without having seen him.

She had been far too astute not to notice the amount of whisky that Gerald consumed during the evening.

She told herself that her father's denunciation of alcohol of all sorts was one of his obsessions and that gentlemen like Lord Hawkston drank wine with their meals as a matter of course.

But Gerald Warren smelt of spirits and, as she saw the tumbler at his right hand being filled again and again by the servants, she knew without being told that he was drinking far too much and that this must account for his appearance.

Besides this, when she was alone in the darkness of her room, the horror of Seetha's death swept over her so that it was difficult to think of anything else.

Dominica loved the Ceylonese women for their gentleness, their sweet natures, their friendliness and the loving childlike trust they had in those they served.

She had real friends amongst those women who attended her father's Church, many of whom came to her with their problems and she knew them intimately.

She could imagine all too vividly Seetha being impressed by Gerald Warren because of his position, because of the fine house he lived in and which must have seemed to her to be luxurious beyond her wildest dreams.

Perhaps, Dominica told herself, she had loved him also with her heart whatever Lord Hawkston might say to the contrary.

Because she knew the people so well she was aware that a Ceylonese peasant who lived in the hill country was a gentleman with a philosophy of life that he was not prepared to barter for material prosperity.

If hunger made it imperative for him to work, he did so and he did it well since he was both skilled and intelligent.

But he preferred to be poor and his own Master rather than rich and at the beck and call of someone else.

Dominica had talked with the women who had come with their husbands into Colombo from many of the outlying provinces, so she knew that the Ceylonese had never become reconciled to the subjugation of their beautiful mountains to the needs of an alien agriculture.

They tried to stand aloof from both the coffee and the tea plantations and Kayons especially, except when they were really hungry, seldom worked on the tea estates in a regular capacity.

This was the reason why the planters had found from the very beginning that it was essential to rely on the importation of Tamil labour who came mostly from the Coramandel coast of Southern India.

It was the Tamils who cleared the jungle and dug the terraces first for coffee and then for the tea that followed it.

Employing Tamil labour made the planters' lives more difficult because they had to learn a new language in order to converse with their labourers, who were not as quick at learning English as were the Ceylonese.

They were happy, easy-going courteous people as a rule and Dominica wondered what agony of mind had forced Seetha into taking her own life.

Could she really have been so unhappy at being turned away by Gerald Warren?

Why did she not seek the comfort of her own people? And why indeed did her father, if he was so fond of her, not prevent her from committing suicide?

There were so many questions that puzzled Dominica and yet she had the feeling that she would never learn the answers because it was a matter that neither Lord Hawkston nor Gerald Warren would ever discuss with her.

Restlessly she rose from her bed, knowing that the dawn must have broken because there was a faint light beneath the curtains.

She drew them back from the window to look out on the view that had held her spellbound the day before.

Her bedroom was at the end of the house and had one long window looking over the valley and another onto the garden and the lake.

The morning mists still shrouded the bottom of the valley, but already there was a faint light glowing behind the mountains in the distance and the stars, which had illuminated the sky the night before, were fading into insignificance.

She turned to the other window and, as she watched the first golden ray of the sun glittered on the cascade as it fell from the hill above down into the lake, she could hear the roar of the torrent as it descended hundreds of feet into the valley shrouded with mist.

It was incredibly lovely and the beauty of the flowers in the garden was breathtaking.

As the light grew stronger, she could see them more clearly, the guelder roses, geraniums and campanulas interspersed with magnolias and oleanders.

There was also feathery bamboo, orchids and mosses, and a number of flowers that she recognised as English such as foxgloves and lobelias, arum lilies and many different species of rose.

With the increasing light Dominica realised that the garden, which must have been laid out with great care by Lord Hawkston, had been allowed to grow wild. Already the jungle of convolvuli, vines and rattans was encroaching upon it and the undergrowth was throttling many of the plants.

She found herself thinking how upset she herself would be if a garden that she had expended so much love and care on should have become neglected during her absence.

She had known without his saying anything the night before that Lord Hawkston had been angry and she was aware that it was only his good manners and self-control which had prevented him from speaking about it at dinner.

It had been bad enough, Dominica thought, that she should feel awkward and shy at meeting Gerald Warren, but what must Lord Hawkston have felt to find his household reorganised, his servants dispersed and his garden neglected?

'He was very brave about it,' she told herself and she wondered if when she had gone to bed he had spoken to his nephew with the anger he had felt inside him.

'He loves this house and everything in it,' Dominica reflected.

Then, almost as if he was a part of her thoughts, she saw Lord Hawkston.

He came from the back of the house and was riding along the farther side of the lake where the torrent passed under a small bridge.

He was on horseback and she saw that he was wearing a white open neck shirt with the sleeves rolled up above his elbows.

He was bareheaded and in his riding breeches he looked young, slim and athletic, very different indeed from his nephew.

Dominica knew that he too must have found it impossible to sleep and so he was riding alone, perhaps to inspect his tea plants or perhaps in search of Lakshman.

At the thought of Seetha and her tragedy Dominica shuddered.

It was hard to think of what she must have suffered before she had thrown herself down the raging torrent to die on the stones that must have been hidden in the mist, even as they were now.

Because she felt that her thoughts were morbid Dominica picked up the wrapper that Madame Fernando had included in her trousseau, put it on over her nightgown and tied the sash of it round her waist.

Made of muslin it was inset with lace and decorated with bows of turquoise-blue ribbon.

It was so attractive and so feminine with lace frills frothing around the hem that Dominica felt that it was almost too grand to be worn in a bedroom.

Then, as she looked around her, she realised that it was in perfect harmony with her surroundings.

It had been difficult last night because she was so confused and shy at meeting Gerald Warren to notice the house properly and yet she had been aware that it was all in exquisite taste such as she had not expected a man might show in furnishings, even if he was proficient at building.

Now she had a confused remembrance of furniture made of the dark ebony which was one of the most prized woods of the Ceylonese cabinet makers and there had also been furniture in satinwood from the magnificent trees which were found all over the island.

In her bedroom now she saw a chest of calamanda, which was stronger and finer than rosewood, and another of nedun, which was highly prized by craftsmen.

The bedroom was lovely and she had learnt when she arrived that all the rooms were known by the names of flowers.

"Where is Dominica sleeping?" Lord Hawkston had enquired of his nephew.

"I told the servants to put her in the 'White Lotus Room'," Gerald replied, "and you are in the one nearby, which I believe you call the 'Red Lotus'."

He spoke in a somewhat contemptuous manner as if he thought that such ideas were ridiculous. But Dominica could understand.

The giant lotus, which was red or white, was so supremely magnificent that it was easy to understand the reverence the people of the East had for this superlative flower.

A botanist had told Dominica that the Hindus believed that the lotus was there before Creation itself and that from its serene perfection all things sprang.

He had shown her the giant lotus and Dominica had seen that the red variety was like a deep red rose reclining on a platform of green floating leaves.

"I have seen vast lakes in the plains," the botanist had said, "where no man has ever been and they have been covered with the lotus, both red and white, which is the flower of Buddha and on which so many of his statues rest."

Dominica was sure now that Lord Hawkston had known this when he designed her bedroom.

The carpet was of deep green like the flat leaves and the back of the bed was carved like the petals of a lotus and painted white just faintly tinged with pink.

The walls were white, tinged with pink where they met the ceiling. The curtains, of textiles blocked and hand-woven by native craftsmen, had the pattern of the lotus woven into them.

They were very lovely, as was the one picture on a wall, which depicted the Buddha surrounded by lotus buds just bursting into flower.

It was exquisitely painted and, as Dominica gazed at it, she felt that its beauty vibrated within her and aroused in her the same feelings that were evoked when she listened to music.

Because she felt unaccountably moved she walked again to the window to look out over the garden wondering if she would still see Lord Hawkston.

But there was only the sunshine now shimmering on the lake and on the cascade and making the brilliance of the flowers in the garden seem even more vivid.

'It is as if one could see them actually growing in the sunshine,' Dominica said to herself.

She looked at the flowers and then again at the valley where the mists were dispersing for so long that she realised time was getting on and she should dress.

There was a bathroom opening out of her bedroom and after she had washed she put on one of the attractive thin muslin gowns that Madame Fernando had called her simple dresses.

They were not simple in Dominica's eyes but she knew that they were becoming and because she wanted to look her best she dressed her hair in a new way, letting it wave softly round her cheeks and then sweeping it backwards in a thick plait that reached from her neck up the very centre of her head.

It was an easy way to dispose of so much hair, but at the same time she knew that it gave her extra height and was becoming.

She had just finished dressing when there came a knock at the door.

"Come in," she called out.

A servant entered, carrying a tray with a small pot of tea, a cup and a jug of milk on it.

"Good morning, *nona*," the servant said, using what Dominica knew was the Portuguese word for 'madam'.

"Good morning," she replied.

"You early, *nona*," the servant remarked with a smile. "I bring tea, but breakfast ready on verandah."

"Then I will have my tea there," Dominica said with a smile.

She allowed the servant to show her the way to the broad verandah outside the dining room where breakfast was laid on a table covered with a white linen cloth.

There was no sign of Lord Hawkston or Gerald and Dominica wondered if she should wait for them.

But the servants had other ideas. They poured out her tea and brought her a slice of pawpaw to start the meal.

Because they obviously expected it Dominica began to eat, but slowly, hoping that Lord Hawkston would appear.

She had not taken more than a few mouthfuls when round the house from the direction of the lake Gerald appeared. He had been swimming and was wearing only shorts and was bare above the waist.

Dominica blushed.

She had never before seen a white man half-naked and she could not help thinking that Gerald looked extremely unprepossessing.

His wet hair was falling over his forehead, his body, fat, hairy and with a decided paunch was sunburnt in red patches.

He carried a large white towel in his hand and Dominica wondered why he did not cover himself with it.

"Good morning, Dominica," he said in a loud voice as he drew nearer. "You are early. I expected that you would be tired this morning."

Dominica rose to her feet a little nervously at his approach.

"I am used to rising early."

"Sit down and get on with your breakfast," Gerald said. "I'll put on a robe and join you in a second."

He walked into the house through an open window and Dominica sat down again.

She could not help noting that his eyes were bloodshot and his face appeared even puffier than it had the night before. She sipped her tea, but somehow she no longer felt hungry.

He returned within a few minutes wearing a long white towelling gown that fastened across his chest, but his neck was bare and, although he had brushed back his hair from his forehead, he still looked unpleasant in Dominica's eyes.

She had a feeling that her father would be shocked at the thought of her sitting down to breakfast with a man wearing nothing but a robe and yet she could not deny that it covered him, and she told herself that it was wrong to criticise or expect those who lived in the wilds of the country to be anything but free and easy.

"Coffee, *Sinna Durai*?" a servant asked at Gerald's elbow.

He hesitated and then enquired,

"Where's the Juggernaut?"

Dominica looked at him in surprise.

"That's a good description of my uncle," he explained as she did not understand. "But if you prefer it, where is the Boss?"

"I saw him go riding some time ago," Dominica answered.

She thought it was extremely bad taste for Gerald to refer to his uncle in such a manner in front of the servants.

"In which case," Gerald said to the servant, "I'll have a whisky and bring it quickly."

Dominica could not help staring at him in surprise. She had never imagined that anyone would want to drink whisky at breakfast.

As if he was aware of her astonishment, Gerald said,

"Might as well indulge myself while I can. Do you know what his Lordship proposed last night?"

"I have no – idea," Dominica replied faintly.

"He told me I had to sign the pledge! Well, I can tell you that if I do, it will be with my fingers crossed and so my oath or vow or whatever it is I take, will mean nothing."

"You mean you will – lie to him?" Dominica enquired.

"Now don't you start!" Gerald exclaimed. "I have had enough preaching for the moment."

The whisky was put down at his side and he drank half the tumbler off in one gulp.

"That's better," he said with a sigh. "Now it will be easier for you and me to have a talk."

Dominica looked at him apprehensively.

She felt that it was hardly the moment for them to talk with two servants in attendance.

But Gerald ignored them as if they were not there, only waving away with a disdainful hand the pawpaw when it was offered to him and looking with a jaundiced eye at a plate of bacon and eggs which was set down in its place.

"If we have to live in this dead-and-alive hole," he said after a moment, "you and I might as well enjoy ourselves. If my skinflint uncle gives us enough money, it's easy to have a bit of fun in Kandy. It's not as good as Colombo, mind you, but they have opened up a decent Club this last year and there are a few convivial people."

"Will you not have to – work on the plantation?" Dominica asked tentatively.

"Not if I can help it!" Gerald answered with one of his raucous laughs. "Of course I shall put on a good show of being interested until the Boss returns to England. I don't suppose he will stay long anyway after we are married. At least I hope not!"

Dominica gripped her fingers together in her lap.

It was not only what Gerald said that was so distressing, but the way he said it. There was something rough and contemptuous in his voice, something that told her that he hated his uncle, just as he hated this beautiful house and the exquisite valley it was situated in.

She tried to visualise to herself what he meant by 'a bit of fun' and only knew instinctively that it was everything she would dislike.

Because she felt that she must say something she asked in a low voice,

"Are there any concerts – in Kandy? Is anyone interested in – music?"

"I shouldn't think so," Gerald replied. "Not unless you mean the type of music one has at a dance. They have one every Saturday night and, although the boys get a bit rough, the girls have fun! There are plenty of opportunities for a cuddle or a kiss in the garden of the Club in the moonlight. Romantic and all that sort of thing. You will enjoy it."

Dominica drew in her breath.

There was really nothing that she could say and she felt as if her brain had gone blank.

Gerald took another swig at his whisky, finishing the glass. He snapped his fingers and a servant replaced it with a full tumbler.

He drank and looked at Dominica as he did so.

"I daresay there are plenty of things I will have to teach you," he said after a moment, his eyes on her face. "But you'll learn. Women learn quickly. I have a feeling we are going to enjoy ourselves you and I."

There was something in the way he spoke and something in the expression on his face that made Dominica feel as if a cobra had suddenly appeared beside her.

Every nerve in her body shrank from him. Even as she longed to run away and yet was afraid to move, she heard a step on the verandah and looked up to see Lord Hawkston approaching them.

She was aware, as a wave of relief swept through her, that Gerald, finishing his whisky in one gulp, had handed the empty glass to a servant who whisked it out of sight in a surreptitious manner.

To Dominica it was degrading that they should contrive together to deceive the owner of the house.

If he noticed what had just occurred Lord Hawkston showed no sign of it.

He had, Dominica saw, changed his shirt since coming in from riding and wore a tie. He was without a coat, but his cuffs were fastened at the wrist with gold links.

"Good morning, Dominica," he said in his quiet deep voice that made her sense of panic subside just because he was there. "Good morning, Gerald. I see you have been swimming."

"Of course," Gerald replied. "It's good for the figure."

"I think you would find it even better exercise if you rode some of the horses in the stable," Lord Hawkston pointed out. "They are under-exercised."

Gerald did not reply. He merely looked sulky.

A servant brought Lord Hawkston a cup of tea.

As he sipped it he said to Dominica,

"It always gives me a sense of satisfaction that is hard to explain in words when I drink my own tea, seated on my own verandah and overlooking my own valley."

"I can understand that," Dominica said with a smile. "And the fact that you are drinking your own tea is more important than anything else."

"It was certainly the foundation stone," Lord Hawkston said. "Did you sleep well?"

Dominica had no wish to tell the truth, but the habit of a lifetime made it impossible to lie.

"I had – a great deal to think about," she said apologetically, "and, of course, I found it – exciting being here."

She felt that this sounded rather inadequate and added,

"The garden is so lovely. I have never seen – such beautiful flowers."

"It *was* lovely," Lord Hawkston said in a low voice and then looking at Gerald he went on, "Need I ask what happened to the gardeners whom I trained with such care?"

"I couldn't afford them!" Gerald replied. "And really, who wants a garden?"

"I do, for one," Lord Hawkston said firmly.

"I can see how many flowers you must have brought here from other countries," Dominica interposed quickly. "But perhaps because I have always lived in Ceylon, I like our own flowers the best."

"The orchids and magnolias," Lord Hawkston smiled.

"And, of course, the lotus."

"They are growing or they were," Lord Hawkston said, "on a pool that I made on the other side of the house.

I will show it to you, but it will be disappointing if the lotuses are no longer there."

"It will indeed," Dominica agreed. "And my bedroom is really beautiful."

"The White Lotus Room," Lord Hawkston said as if to himself. "I was fortunate in finding craftsmen who could really carve. I must show you the bedrooms on the next floor. The 'Palm Room', where they copied the Areca Palms, is, in my opinion, unique."

"I would love to see it," Dominica exclaimed.

"I think before we do anything else," Lord Hawkston said, looking at his nephew, "we should pay a visit to the plantation.

I want you to show me, Gerald, the work that has been done and any innovations that have been put in hand these last two years."

"I expect you will find it just as you left it," Gerald answered.

"I hope so," Lord Hawkston replied. "If you will get dressed, I will order the horses. Dominica can come with us. She has ridden in the past and will find the horse I rode this morning not too obstreperous now that I have exercised him."

Dominica looked at him anxiously.

"I don't want to be in the way."

"You will not be. Put on your habit. We ordered a light one from Madame Fernando and now is the right moment to try it out."

Dominica flashed him a smile and ran to her bedroom.

She had been afraid when she heard Lord Hawkston making his plans that she would be left behind, but now he was taking her with them and her heart was singing with excitement at the thought of seeing the plantation that meant so much to him.

It only took her a few minutes to take off her muslin gown and put on an attractive habit that Madame Fernando had made her in pink cotton decorated with white braid.

There was a straw hat to wear with it and Dominica was pleased to find that she was ready quicker than Gerald and that Lord Hawkston was waiting alone in the hall when she joined him.

"You will not be afraid to ride?" he asked as she appeared. "I promise you that the horse I rode this morning is really quite a peaceful animal."

"I don't think I have forgotten how to ride, even though it was five years ago since I last did so," Dominica answered.

"I think it is something one never forgets," Lord Hawkston said reassuringly.

They walked outside the house as they were speaking to find the horses waiting for them.

Lord Hawkston lifted Dominica into the saddle.

She had a strange feeling as he put his hands on her waist that she could not explain to herself.

She only knew that it was there and that she wanted to ride well so that he would be proud of her.

She picked up the reins and he smiled encouragingly.

"I see you have not forgotten."

"I hope I shall not – disgrace myself."

"You could never do that."

She was looking down at him because she was seated on the horse and he was standing beside her.

She realised perhaps for the first time that his eyes were a very deep blue. It seemed to her that they were even more vivid because already his skin seemed to have tanned a little.

Her eyes looked into his.

Then Lord Hawkston looked away.

"Are you sure the stirrup is the right length?" he asked and Dominica had difficulty in understanding what he said.

"Yes – yes – quite all right," she answered.

Lord Hawkston mounted the other horse.

"We may as well start. Gerald can catch us up."

"Will he know where to go?" Dominica enquired.

"I imagine so."

They rode off taking the path that wound its way down the hillside into a valley below.

Lord Hawkston set the pace and the horses moved slowly.

Dominica began to get her confidence back, but a full-grown horse was rather different from the pony she had ridden as a child.

She remembered how she had longed to enter for the Gymkhana, which was one of the annual amusements of the other children in Colombo, but her father had never allowed it, even though her mother pleaded with him.

"You can attend if you have nothing better to do," he conceded grudgingly.

But he had not allowed them to compete, even though Dominica had known that there were several competitions which either she or Faith could have won.

Now she wondered if such deprivations had made them better people in any way or indeed better Christians.

Why should religion always be so gloomy and so austere?

Why must laughter and happiness always be frowned on by the God her father worshipped?

Then she stopped being introspective because Lord Hawkston was explaining to her about the tea.

"Tea is the one crop that can be picked six days out of seven all the year round," he told her, "with the exception of two or three of the great Hindu festivals."

Before they reached the coolies working amongst the tea plants Dominica could already hear them.

"The Tamils are noisy and very often quarrelsome," Lord Hawkston said as she looked at him as if for explanation. "But they are good workers."

They drew nearer and Dominica could see that the tea pluckers had large round bamboo baskets slung onto their backs by means of a rope that passed around their foreheads.

The women wore gaily coloured cloths wound Grecian fashion across their breasts and round their heads and padded where they took the strain of the rope on their foreheads, they wore a headcloth like a turban.

In green, red, gold or white the effect of a hundred or more pluckers waist-high in greenery was, Dominica thought, very picturesque.

She was fascinated by the speed and skill of the women picking the ripe leaves, always two and a bud, and gathering them in small heaps in the hand, then throwing them with a lithe quick jerk over their shoulders into the waiting basket.

"The supervision of the work is in the hands of the men," Lord Hawkston explained. "They are called *Kanganies* or Overseers."

There was a faint smile on his lips as he looked at them and it was with difficulty that Dominica prevented herself from laughing.

The insignia of their rank was usually an ancient European-type jacket, a turban and an umbrella, a high sign of superiority, caught in the collar of the coat and hanging down their backs.

"Four times a day," Lord Hawkston went on, "the leaf is carefully weighed, each plucker's tally being entered in a small account book by the *kannackapiller*."

He looked at the pluckers with an expression of pride in his eyes.

"There is never any cheating. If the accounts are challenged, the coolies' recording, for they know exactly how much they have picked, can be accepted as completely accurate."

Everyone seemed to be very happy and it was impossible not to notice how delighted many of the coolies were to see Lord Hawkston.

There was a note of pleasure in their voices when he talked to them and Dominica was sure that they had a genuine fondness for him.

It was very different when a little while later Gerald came trotting up to them.

He was looking hot and the perspiration was running down his face.

With what Dominica thought was an effort to impress his uncle he dismounted and walked round to the pluckers finding fault with their work and speaking to them in a tone of voice that made her instinctively grip the reins tighter.

No one answered back, everyone went on working, but Dominica was sure that they resented Gerald's hectoring manner, the loudness of his orders and his whole attitude of arrogant superiority.

They watched the weighing of the tea outside a store that, Lord Hawkston told Dominica, had originally been built for coffee.

All too soon it seemed to Dominica time passed and they rode back along a different route towards the house.

Gerald was blustering and making long and garbled explanations as to why the tea production had fallen in the last year.

He blamed the coolies, the Overseers, the weather, the plants themselves, while in fact, Dominica was sure that it was all a cover-up for his own inadequacy.

Lord Hawkston said little, but she knew that he was feeling disappointed and upset that the plantation he had left in such excellent condition, thriving and improving month by month, should have gone backwards instead of forwards and would undoubtedly show a financial deficit instead of a profit.

After a time, when his words evoked no response from his uncle, Gerald's voice ceased, and Dominica was glad to ride in silence and look at the beauty all around her.

She was fascinated to see that where the country had not been cultivated the jungle was even more beautiful than she had imagined it could be.

There were varieties of immense feathery bamboos and she noticed low down in the valley giant fern trees rising sometimes to a height of more than twenty feet.

Almost everywhere in the thick undergrowth there was the vivid blue of the nelu in a great sheet of colour and besides the magnolias there were myrtles and various varieties of camellia.

When she was looking at one, entranced by the perfect waxlike blossoms, Lord Hawkston followed the direction of her eyes and said,

"You know, of course. that the tea plant is a cousin of the camellia?"

"No, I did not," Dominica answered him, "but now that you mention it, they do look rather similar."

"Let me show you something even more beautiful," he suggested.

They rode on for a little distance and then he pointed to the *katu-imbul* or silk-cotton tree.

Dominica had seen one in the gardens in Colombo, but here there were a dozen of them growing wild and the glorious trumpet-like petals were in an almost crazy profusion.

The ground beneath the trees was carpeted thick with petals like a crimson rug and the branches of the trees grew out at right angles from the trunk like the yards of a ship.

It was so lovely that she could hardly bear to leave it behind and ride on, but she told herself that whatever happened she must come again before the blossom finished.

They reached the house and Lord Hawkston said as he lifted her down from the saddle,

"You may think that we have returned early, but here as men breakfast soon after dawn it is usual for the midday meal to be at noon."

"Whatever the time is," Dominica said with a smile, "I am hungry."

This was true because she had been unable to eat any breakfast as Gerald Warren had upset her.

Now she tried to tell herself that she was being stupid and ultra-fastidious. He was Lord Hawkston's nephew and she must try to understand him.

'He is feeling awkward, as I am, about the arrangements that have been made for us,' she thought.

It sounded reassuring and sensible, but she knew that inside she shrank with every nerve in her body from the idea that she should mean anything to this hard-drinking young man or he to her.

After luncheon Lord Hawkston insisted that Dominica should rest.

"It is always a mistake to do too much on the first day," he said. "The height, although one does not realise it, affects one after coming up from sea level. Besides Gerald and I are going for a long ride that will be too much for you."

She was disappointed, but she could not help recognising that he was being wise. In fact when she went to her room she lay down on the bed meaning to read one of the many books that she had found waiting for her, but fell asleep.

She had not slept the night before and now she slept peacefully to find when she awoke that it was six o'clock in the evening.

"You should have wakened me," she told the servant when she rang for him to find out the exact time.

"*Durai* say you should sleep, *nona*," he replied. "You like bath?"

"Thank you," Dominica smiled.

By the time she had had her bath it was getting on for seven o'clock and she put on one of the pretty evening gowns that Madame Fernando had included in her trousseau.

Pale yellow, it was the colour of syringa, the bodice fitted her closely and was cut low at the front and at the back. There were tiny puff sleeves fashioned of yellow tulle, which was also draped round the full skirt.

It seemed very grand and very décolletée for a quiet evening in the hills, but Dominica hoped that Lord Hawkston would admire her in it.

Feeling a little shy she went into the sitting room.

It was a long and very lovely room filled with treasures of native craftsmanship, which Dominica was longing to inspect.

To her disappointment she found not Lord Hawkston but Gerald and he was alone.

He had a glass of whisky in his hand and looked up apprehensively when she entered as if he thought it might be his uncle.

"Oh, it's you, Dominica," he exclaimed. "You are early! I have not yet changed for dinner."

"Did you enjoy your ride?" Dominica asked, crossing the room towards him.

"Not much," he replied. "I felt like a small boy who had forgotten to do his homework!"

For the first time Dominica felt rather sympathetic towards him.

"Was his Lordship very angry?" she asked.

"I am in disgrace you know that. But don't let's worry our heads about it. There are other things we can do besides sit in sackcloth and ashes."

He put down his glass and said unexpectedly,

"For instance you could start by giving me a kiss. We are going to be married, Dominica, but so far we have not had a chance of getting to know each other."

He put out his arms as he spoke and pulled her roughly towards him.

Instinctively and without conscious thought she struggled and fought herself free.

"No!" she cried. "*No!*"

There was a tremor of fear in her voice.

"Why not?" Gerald asked. "Are you playing hard to get, Dominica? After all, you have come here to marry me."

"Yes – I know," Dominica said breathlessly, "but it is too – soon. We have only – just met. I-I have hardly spoken to you."

"That's not my fault. And now that I have had a chance to look at you, I can say you are very pretty! What's more, you have a very white skin. I like that. It's a change!"

As he spoke, he put his arms round Dominica again and kissed her bare shoulder.

It happened so swiftly that she was unable to move away or prevent it. Then, as she felt the touch of his lips, she realised what he had said.

"It's a change!"

A change from Seetha – a change from the girl who had killed herself because of him.

Even as her whole being was revolted at the thought, Dominica felt his lips hot and greedy on her bare skin.

"No! *No!*" she cried again and parted her lips to scream.

As she did so, the door opened and Lord Hawkston entered the room.

He had changed for dinner and, although he must have seen what was happening as he came towards them, his voice was completely expressionless.

"You will be late, Gerald, if you don't hurry."

Gerald took his arms from Dominica and she felt for one moment that she was going to faint.

She put out her hands and just beside her there was the back of a chair and she held onto it.

"I won't be long," Gerald said and walked away.

Dominica fought for breath.

She had her back to Lord Hawkston and did not turn round.

She only knew that she felt a great relief because he was there and at the same time a sense of acute embarrassment because he had seen Gerald kissing her bare shoulder.

What did he think? How could he credit that she would permit such a thing?

Then she told herself that it was what he would expect. He had brought her here to marry his nephew and he would be glad that they were getting to know each other and that Gerald was attracted to her.

Even as she thought of him she could feel the heat of his lips, could smell his spirit-laden breath and could feel the roughness of his arms as he pulled her against him.

'I cannot – do it!' she told herself. 'I must – tell Lord Hawkston that I – cannot do it.'

She heard him walk across the room to the window.

"Have you seen the sunset?" he asked in a quiet voice.

It checked the words that would have sprung to Dominica's lips, words in which she would have explained how Gerald revolted her, how she could never let him touch her again and how she could not stay here.

Then, as if someone was pointing an accusing finger at her, she remembered all that she owed Lord Hawkston!

Her whole trousseau, which had cost an astronomical sum, gowns and bonnets for the girls, the kindness he had shown to her as they travelled here and how he was doing everything to make her feel at home.

'How can I be so – ungrateful? How can I explain that I must break my word and – go back on my – promise?' Dominica asked herself.

She felt the faintness that had come over her when Gerald released her was now passing, but she was still conscious of his lips on her shoulder where he had kissed her.

She still felt a kind of sick depression inside but she told herself that she had to be brave.

What else could she do, owing Lord Hawkston so much? And being so desperately and hopelessly in his debt?

'If I worked for a hundred years, I could never pay him back for all he has spent on me,' she thought.

With an effort that was superhuman she walked towards him.

As she reached his side, he stepped forward through the open window and out onto the Verandah.

"Sometimes I think that this is the loveliest part of the day," he said. "When I lived here alone I always used to try to be back in time to watch the sun go down and the stars come out. It is more beautiful and more moving than any play in a theatre could be and the sounds of the night have a music that to me are finer than the greatest opera."

Dominica knew that he was trying to soothe and reassure her. He was attempting, she was sure, to tell her that if she did not panic, if she used her common sense, then everything would be all right.

But would it?

Would she ever be able to endure Gerald near her, to feel him touching her and to let him kiss her?

She reached out her hand to hold onto one of the pillars of the verandah and saw that it was trembling.

'How can I tell him the – truth?' she asked herself and knew that it was impossible.

CHAPTER SIX

It was another uncomfortable evening with Lord Hawkston trying to make conversation and receiving little response from either Dominica or his nephew.

Dominica did make an effort, but she found that it was increasingly hard to chatter and smile and impossible to prevent herself from shuddering when she looked at Gerald.

It seemed to her, however, that Lord Hawkston was quite unaware that there was an undercurrent to the conversation nor did he seem to notice that Gerald had imbibed a great deal of whisky before he came back to the sitting room dressed for dinner.

During the meal he ostentatiously drank the fresh lime juice that had been prepared for Dominica, but after dinner when he left the room for a few minutes, she was sure that it was because he was seeking another drink.

They had coffee on the verandah and by now the sky was darkening and the stars were coming out one by one.

There was a faint glow over the valley and she knew that in the depths of it the mists would be rising to cast a gossamer film over the tea plants.

There was the sound of the torrent and the cry of the night birds besides the shrill note of the 'flying-foxes'.

These tiny bats, hardly larger than a thumbnail, swooped around the verandah as if they were inquisitive. Whenever the nights came on in a Ceylonese house they appeared in a flock, lured by some mysterious attraction.

The moths, however, were too numerous for the party to linger long on the verandah and soon they returned to the sitting room.

Lord Hawkston talked to Dominica for some time about the furniture that he had had made in different parts of the country and which had been brought to his house by various different means. One piece had been carried on the back of an elephant!

All the time he was talking Dominica was conscious of Gerald sprawled in an armchair, doubtless wondering how soon he could obtain another drink without his uncle being aware of it.

It was not yet ten o'clock when she decided that she would go to bed.

She bade both gentlemen good night, curtseying as she did so and then went to her room feeling that it was a relief to be alone.

At the same time she would have liked to go on talking to Lord Hawkston.

She undressed and was ready for bed. Then having blown out the light she pulled back the curtains and opened the long windows onto the verandah that overlooked the lake.

The garden was very quiet and peaceful. In the light from the starlit sky the water of the lake was luminous and the fragrance of the flowers almost overpowering.

'It is lovely – so incredibly lovely!' Dominica told herself. 'If only one could be here with someone – "

She checked the thought before it went any further.

What was the point of wishing for the impossible?

If she stayed, she must stay with Gerald as his wife.

She turned back into the bedroom as if the beauty outside hurt her.

She crept into bed closing her eyes to try not to remember what she had felt when he had touched her, when he had kissed the whiteness of her skin and said with incredible insensitivity,

"*It's a change!*"

How was it possible, she asked herself, for her ever to forget Seetha and that she had killed herself because this man had turned her away?

'I will not think of it – *I will not*!' Dominica told herself.

And yet she felt almost as if Seetha was beside her, talking to her and telling her how much she had suffered.

Suddenly Dominica knew the reason why Seetha had killed herself.

It was because she was too ashamed at being turned away without any money to return to her village!

It would mean that no man would marry her without a dowry. She could not face the scorn of her friends and relations and knew herself to be a failure.

Death was preferable to disgrace and the torrent made death easy!

'How could Gerald have done that to her?' Dominica asked the darkness.

*

As Dominica left the sitting room, Lord Hawkston said to his nephew,

"I have something to tell you, Gerald."

"What is it?"

"I rose early this morning," Lord Hawkston answered, "and I rode over to the village where Lakshman lives. I hoped to see him, but he was not there. However I discovered some important facts about him."

Gerald did not answer. He only looked at his uncle with a surly expression on his face as if he resented his intrusion into what he obviously felt were his own private affairs.

"The villagers told me that Lakshman has been struck by the Rakshyos with madness."

"What the devil does that mean?" Gerald enquired.

Lord Hawkston made an impatient gesture.

"You have been in this country for two years. Surely you have tried to understand something about these people? Especially those in the hill country who you are dealing with."

"If you are referring to their religious beliefs, I cannot make head or tail of such rigmarole!"

The way he spoke made Lord Hawkston tighten his lips, but in a quiet voice he answered,

"You must be aware that, although the Ceylonese are Buddhists, the villagers still depend in many ways on the Hindu Gods. They believe in good and bad omens and in evil spirits and demons, which were the beliefs of their Yakkho forebears."

Looking at his nephew Lord Hawkston realised that he was not particularly interested, but he continued,

"They are in fact still devil worshippers and even their worship of a peaceful gentle Buddha does not prevent this. Cruelty and death, sickness and pain are all in the hands of legions of devils and spirits that the unseen world teems with."

Lord Hawkston paused and there was a smile on his lips as he added,

"There is, in point of fact, in my opinion, very little difference between the spirits and devils of the Ceylonese and the doctrine of Satan and Hell that is preached so fervently in Colombo by Dominica's father."

"You told me he is a Parson," Gerald said. "Why, in Heaven's name, did you choose me a Parson's brat for a wife?"

"I chose Dominica," Lord Hawkston said and now his voice was cold, "because she has both personality and character, something that I am sorry to see is singularly lacking where you are concerned."

"You have made that obvious," Gerald said with a snarl in his voice. "Go on with your lecture."

Lord Hawkston ignored the rudeness in his tone.

"The good spirits of the villagers," he continued, "are the Yakshyos, who are kind and gentle with a veneration for the Lord Buddha.

"On the other hand the Rakshyos are fierce, malevolent and evil. They inhabit the places of the dead and forests, where each has his own particular tree from where he will strike a passer-by with madness!"

Lord Hawkston walked across the room before he carried on,

"This may seem strange and far-fetched to you and me, but the people here believe it, and they told me with all sincerity that Lakshman has been driven mad by a Rakshyo."

"Then bad luck to him!" Gerald said lightly. "I cannot see that I can do anything about it."

"It is more serious than you seem to imagine," Lord Hawkston retorted sharply.

"Why?"

"You have been here during the Ceylonese New Year and you must know, if you have taken the slightest interest in our people, that the long anticipated festival, which is a time of family reunion all over the island, brings in its train a great number of evils, particularly gambling and drinking."

Lord Hawkston glanced at his nephew as he spoke and continued evenly,

"Under the stress of such excitement the excitable side of the Ceylonese nature overcomes their habitual gentleness and passivity. Quarrels flare up suddenly, stabbings are frequent and, as you may not be aware, the murder rate in Ceylon is very high."

"Are you suggesting," Gerald asked, "that Lakshman will murder me?"

"I consider it quite a possibility," Lord Hawkston answered. "The *Kappurala*, or the Devil Dancer, in the village whose job it is to cast out or placate evil spirits spoke very seriously of Lakshman. He knows his own people and I am prepared to listen to his warnings."

"Well, I am not!" Gerald exclaimed positively. "If you ask me, the whole thing is a lot of nauseating rubbish thought up by the Priests to extort money from the fools who listen to them. I know Lakshman. I met him when he came to offer me his daughter. He is a quiet inoffensive chap about half my size. I am no more afraid of him than I would be of a strutting bantam cock!"

"Very well," Lord Hawkston said. "I have now arranged for a thorough search to be made for Lakshman so that I can pay him the money you owe him and try in some fashion to compensate him for the loss of his daughter. All I can say is that your behaviour in the matter and your callous indifference to the death of this wretched girl appals me."

As if he was afraid that he might say anymore Lord Hawkston went from the sitting room closing the door behind him.

His nephew sat still for a few seconds and then he clapped his hands to summon a servant to bring him a glass of whisky that he felt in vital need of.

*

Dominica was dreaming.

In her dream she heard Prudence crying.

Sometimes, after their mother had died Prudence had suffered from nightmares from which she had awoken calling for her mother, only to burst into floods of tears when she found that she was not there. Dominica had always left the door of her and Faith's room open so that they would hear Prudence if she cried out since she slept on the other side of the passage.

It had been a desperate loss for all the sisters when Mrs. Radford had died, but Prudence had only been seven and she had missed her mother with an intensity that made Dominica fear at times that her sorrow would undermine her health.

It is true that she had never been very strong. She had been born prematurely and, from the time she was a baby, she had been small, pale and more prone to sickness than the others.

Perhaps because she was the weakest one of the family Mrs. Radford had seemed to love her the most and yet none of her other children had been jealous.

Prudence, they felt, was someone special and Dominica had decided when she left Colombo that the first person she would have to stay with her in her new home would be not Hope but Prudence.

She was well aware that Prudence's sensitive nature found it hard to endure the harshness of her father's religion and his attitude towards them.

He disciplined them all as if he felt that they were sinners who must be purged of evil and for Prudence to be included in this general condemnation was, Dominica knew, bad for her not only mentally but also physically.

She had been thinking of Prudence before she fell asleep tonight and wondering how she, or her other sisters, would fit into the household.

She had fondly imagined before she arrived that Gerald Warren would both look like his uncle and also be kind and understanding as Lord Hawkston had been ever since she knew him.

But now not only her own dreams of the life she might lead were fading but also her plans for her sisters were evaporating like the mists over the valley.

What would Faith think of Gerald's drinking?

She was certain that Charity with her sharp intelligence would see at once that he treated the workers in the wrong way and might even find out the truth about Seetha.

That was an episode, Dominica told herself, that the girls must never learn about.

She knew only too well how shocked and horrified they would be, because like her they loved the gentle, attractive Ceylonese women.

EquallyDominica was aware that the air here in the mountains would suit Prudence and perhaps bring some colour into her pale cheeks.

She would enjoy the meals, because whomever else he dismissed Gerald had kept his uncle's superlative cook and Dominica found every dish a delight that she had never before experienced.

Now half-asleep she sat up in bed thinking that she must go to Prudence and comfort her.

And then she realised where she was.

She was not in the Vicarage but miles away from her family and the cry she thought had come from Prudence was obviously from some animal out in the garden.

It came very clearly through the window she had opened onto the verandah and now more fully awake she realised that it was not a cry but a whimper or whine that a very small animal might make.

She was well aware that many animals in the jungle made strange sounds. She had read books on how travellers had been frightened almost out of their wits by jackals whose cries are so blood-curdling that they strike a chill to the heart.

There was no reason to be afraid or upset by the little whimper she heard and yet somehow as it continued it was rather sinister and she was sure that the animal, whatever it was, was just outside the window.

'It will move away in a moment,' Dominica told herself and lay down again.

But it was impossible not to hear the continuous sound. It was piteous, so that Dominica knew that it would be impossible to sleep again as long as it continued.

'It will go away in a moment,' she told herself again. 'It would be ridiculous for me to try to help the animal.'

Perhaps it was in pain, but it was very unlikely, even if it was, that it would allow her to go near it.

'I will not listen,' Dominica determined and she turned her head sideways onto the pillow.

Nevertheless she knew that she was still tense as the whining continued.

She wished now that she had not left her bedroom window open.

Supposing it came into the room? Supposing, worse than the plaintive animal, a snake came in from the verandah?

She felt her heart begin to thump in fright.

Then suddenly, there was a snarling noise that made her leap with fear.

There could be no pretending that this was not a savage animal and one that was definitely dangerous! The snarling became a roar and the sound seemed duplicated and the intensity of it was deafening.

For a moment Dominica was paralysed with fear. Then in a panic that swept away every thought and every feeling except that of a terror, which shot through her like the sharpness of steel, she sprang from her bed and running across the room pulled open the door.

She had no idea where she was going, she was past thought, past everything but a horror that drove her instinctively with a sense of self-preservation to run away.

She opened another door and ran quickly, wildly and frantically, to where she knew that she would be safe.

*

Lord Hawkston had also been awakened by the noise and he knew at once that it was two leopards fighting. As he awoke, he cursed his nephew once again for his indolence and indifference to what was the ordinary duty of a planter.

The leopards had at one time been so prolific in the jungles of Ceylon that they had proved a real menace to the tea planters.

With their numbers kept under control, they had become rarer and were not dangerous to man under normal circumstances.

They brought down deer and cattle and exercised mesmeric power on the monkeys whom they seemed to regard as their natural enemies.

But, if a planter allowed the wild beasts of the jungle to encroach upon his plantation and become a menace, not so much to the workers, as to their animals, like pigs and dogs, he had no one to blame but himself.

As Lord Hawkston sat up, he wondered if the leopards would remain in the garden long enough for him to find a gun and shoot them.

Then, even as he thought about it someone small and terrified came through the door of his room and running towards the bed flung herself upon him.

His arms went round Dominica and he knew as she pressed herself against him that she was trembling all over and he realised how frightened she must be.

"It's all right," he said quietly. "They will not harm you."

Her hands clutching at his nightshirt were convulsive and he felt her press herself even closer as if she sought sanctuary from the fears that beset her.

"It sounds very terrifying," Lord Hawkston said in his calm deep voice, "but at this time of the year, when the animals are mating, there are frequently fights in the jungle and the wild elephants make the most noise of them all!"

He realised as he spoke that his words were having little effect upon Dominica.

She was still trembling convulsively and her face was hidden against his shoulder.

"The leopards are still there. Let me go and find a gun, Dominica. I will shoot them and they will never worry you again."

"No – *no*! Don't – leave me!"

Her voice was low, but he heard the panic in it.

"I will not do anything that will upset you further," he said, "but you must be sensible about this."

He got no further.

"I am not – sensible I never – have been – sensible!" Dominica cried. "I have – tried to be what you – wanted, but it's – impossible! I am frightened of – everything. I have tried to – hide it but it is no good."

"That is not true," Lord Hawkston said. "I think you have been very brave about many things."

"I am – not, *I am – not*!" Dominica persisted. "I have been – acting a lie, but you have not – realised it. I have been – afraid ever since I was a child. I was afraid of – angels, so Papa made me stay all – night in the – Church alone and now I am – afraid of the dark! I am afraid of – snakes and of – leopards. I am afraid of – Mr. Warren and of having to – marry him!"

The words were said in a passionate whisper, but they were said and Lord Hawkston knew as he listened that he might have expected them.

"You will despise me – I know you will," Dominica went on, "and I am – afraid of making you – angry. But you have to – know the truth and I am – ashamed that I have – deceived you."

She burst into tears as she spoke and Lord Hawkston felt the tempest that racked her thin body. It made him feel as if he held a very young and very unhappy child in his arms.

For a moment there was nothing he could say. He could only hold her close as she wept despairingly and hopelessly, as if she no longer had any control over her emotions.

She must have bottled up her feelings for so long, Lord Hawkston thought, that now it was like a dam that had broken and her pent-up emotions were sweeping everything away in a flood leaving her nothing but her sense of insecurity.

"Don't cry, Dominica," he urged gently at last. "I will put everything right for you. It is not as bad as you think."

"It – is! It *is*!" Dominica murmured in between her tears. "I have – let you down. I have broken my promise, but I cannot – help it. I am such a – coward – such a hopeless and – despicable coward!"

"You are nothing of the sort," Lord Hawkston insisted.

His nightshirt was now soaked with her tears, but he was aware that she was not trembling so violently in his arms.

Then suddenly he realised that there was no longer any sounds from outside.

"The leopards have gone," he told her. "I am sorry in a way you could not have seen them because the Ceylon leopard is a very fine and impressive creature. There are black rings round his body rather like a tiger, but much less clearly marked. He has spots only upon his legs and his spring, which is enormous, is one of the most graceful movements in the whole animal world."

He was talking deliberately to divert Dominica's mind from her misery and as he went on he knew that she was listening to him.

"There is also a pure black leopard on the island. He is very beautiful, but I have seen only three of them all the years I have been in Ceylon."

Dominica gave a little sigh.

Her tears ceased, but she did not move her face away from Lord Hawkston's shoulder.

He knew that she had turned to him in her terror entirely for protection.

She had forgotten that she was wearing only a thin muslin nightgown, one of the beautifully embroidered ones that Madame Fernando had included in her trousseau.

She was not even aware that Lord Hawkston was in fact a man.

He was everything that was safe, a stronghold against terror, a sanctuary against fear, a protection against anything that might hurt her.

He was in fact quite impersonal and yet she had turned to him because he was the one man whom she knew that she needed at this particular moment.

"Everything is quiet," Lord Hawkston said softly.

Dominica raised her head.

He could not see her in the darkness, but he could feel her long hair trailing over her shoulders and falling well below her waist.

She smelt of a flower that for a moment he could not identify. Then he realised that it was in fact the sweet fragrance of lavender.

It was a strangely English scent amongst all the exotic perfumes of the East and somehow it made him think of all he loved in England and of his mother.

"You need no longer be afraid, Dominica," he said gently.

"I am – not," she replied, but her voice caught in her throat as she spoke and sounded somehow infinitely pathetic like a very young child's.

"Tomorrow I will make certain that the leopards do not disturb you again," Lord Hawkston promised. "I will have the bedrooms opened up on the next floor. I should have insisted on it as soon as I arrived,"

"I would feel – safer up there," Dominica said, "but not if I was – alone."

"My bedroom is there," Lord Hawkston answered. "The one I built for myself. The 'Palm Room', but you know, wherever you might be, that I would protect you."

"That is – why I came to – find you," Dominica whispered.

Her face was no longer hidden against his shoulder, but she made no effort to move from the protection of his arms.

He was aware that even while she tried to speak naturally she was still tense, still listening, as if she feared that the savage sounds of the leopards might break out again.

"I wanted you to have a good night," he said. "You have been tired and perhaps upset by many things since we left Colombo."

"I – could not go back to – that room."

"No, of course not," he agreed. "We will change places. You can sleep here and I will keep a watch for the leopards. But I promise you, they will not return."

"Don't – leave me yet," Dominica begged. "Not for a – moment."

He felt her hand tighten once again on his nightshirt.

"I will not leave you until you tell me to do so, but I think you ought to try to sleep. So what I am going to suggest is that you get into bed and I will stay beside you until it is dawn or until you are asleep."

"You must – think I am very – foolish," Dominica muttered with a little sob.

"I think you did exactly the right thing in coming to find me when you were frightened."

Very gently he took his arms from her. Then, as she sat up on the bed where she had been lying against him, he stepped out onto the floor and put out his hands to find his dressing gown, which was lying over an adjacent chair.

He put it on and, as he did so, Dominica climbed into bed and pulled the sheet over her.

"You will – not go away yet – will you?" she stammered.

Lord Hawkston sat down on the bed and putting out his hands found hers.

"I promise you I will stay."

She gave a little sigh as if of relief. Then her fingers tightened on his.

"Are you – very angry with – me?"

"I am not angry, I don't despise you and I don't think that you in the least foolish," he answered. "I think, as I have always thought, that you are a very exceptional and very brave person."

"I am not – you know I am not!" Dominica said. "But I like you to – think so."

"I promise you I am speaking the truth."

There was a silence and then he said,

"Close your eyes, Dominica. I think you will find it easier to fall asleep and actually there is very little of the night left. I don't need to look at my watch to tell you that in under half an hour the dawn will be breaking over the mountains, bringing us another golden day of sunshine."

He felt her fingers relax beneath his.

She did not move and after a very short while he heard her breathing evenly.

He had known that she had exhausted herself both by fear and with her tears and he had been certain that once she relaxed she would sleep quickly and deeply as he had seen men sleep after some abnormal exertion or emotional stress.

He did not move but sat very still, his hands still on Dominica's until, as he had expected, there was a faint light between the curtains as they stirred with the dawn breeze.

Still Lord Hawkston waited. Then, as it grew lighter, he could see first the outline of the furniture in the room and then Dominica's face against the pillows.

Her hair covered her shoulders and he could see that her eyelashes were still wet as they lay dark against the pale cheeks of her little heart-shaped face.

She looked very young and very defenceless and Lord Hawkston looked at her for a long time. Then gently he disengaged his hands from hers and, rising, moved silently across the room to the half-open door.

He passed through it and closed it very quietly behind him.

He walked along the passage and entered Dominica's room. He saw the bedclothes thrown back as she had left them when she ran away and the window open onto the verandah.

He walked through it. The lawn where the leopards had fought was scratched up, flowers were broken and plants were lying with their roots in the air.

Lord Hawkston stood looking at the damage and then his eyes dropped to the edge of the verandah.

Attached to one of the supporting pillars was a piece of broken string that would have held captive a small animal such as the kid of a spotted deer!

Lord Hawkston stared at the thickly covered hills. Somewhere hidden in them Lakshman was waiting to avenge his daughter's death.

If Dominica had gone to the assistance of the frightened kid last night, the leopards would have attacked her!

He now recognised that he must find Lakshman and quickly.

*

When Dominica awoke and found herself in a strange room and in another bed, the events of the night before came flooding back to her.

She glanced at the clock that stood beside the bed and realised that it was late and she had slept well into the morning.

It was not surprising. At the same time she felt ashamed of her own weakness and shy when she remembered that she had driven Lord Hawkston from his bed because she had been so terrified.

'How could I have been so stupid?' she asked herself.

But even to think of the dreadful noise of the leopards in the darkness was to feel a renewed tremor of fear.

She had been truthful when she told Lord Hawkston that she had always been timid. She had forced herself not to show it, because she knew that she must set an example to her younger sisters, but she had never forgotten the terrible experience her father had made her undergo when she was only seven years old.

Her mother being ill at the time had not realised what was happening, although afterwards she had been very angry.

Her father had been giving her a scripture lesson when he had talked of angels guarding people and saving them from the devils that existed in Hell.

He made it all seem very vivid and very real to the child he was teaching and as usual he was carried away by his own oratory and had described Hell in such colourful terms that Dominica had cried,

"I am frightened of devils, Papa, I am frightened – they will catch hold of me."

"You will be safe as long as you are good," her father replied. "God sends his angels to protect you and angels are always around you, Dominica, saving you from sin."

"I am frightened of angels – too," Dominica had replied. "I don't want anything around me – I want to be alone!"

The Vicar had looked on this as sacrilege and had rebuked Dominica. Because even at seven years old she had a great deal of spirit she had defied him.

"I am afraid of angels. Papa, whatever you may say about them – I am, *I am*!"

It ended in her being shut in the Church all night so that she could meditate on the angels and realise that she was safe in God's hands.

Dominica remembered it all vividly and how the darkness had seemed peopled not with angels but with devils.

Finally in her terror she had crouched down on the floor in the Governor's pew, making herself as small as possible and put her hands over her ears in case she should hear the angels talking to her.

They found her in the morning asleep from sheer exhaustion with her head on one of the crimson hassocks.

The Vicar had never inflicted such a punishment on any of his other children. He had been far too afraid of his wife's anger.

But it had given Dominica a sense of insecurity that she had never lost. It had made her afraid of the dark so that it had always been a comfort to have Faith sharing a room with her.

She had, however, as she was the eldest, forced herself to assume authority and when her mother died she tried to take her place not only with her sisters but also with her father.

It was not always easy where he was concerned, but she could sometimes soften the strictness of his orders or divert him from his most austere demands on them.

Only when it came to obtaining money from him for payment for food and other necessities did she admit to herself that she was a hopeless failure.

At the same time she had never in her life behaved quite so weakly or, she thought, so humiliatingly as she had last night.

She was aware that it must have been the culmination of many things, shock at Lord Hawkston's proposition, unhappiness at leaving home, the revulsion that she had felt when she met Gerald and most of all the horror of his lips when he had kissed her shoulder and the terror that she felt for the future.

She wondered what Lord Hawkston was thinking about her this morning and whether he regretted having brought her with him to the house he had built himself.

If he had thought her worthy of living here, if he had imagined her as its hostess and chatelaine, surely now he would be terribly disillusioned at finding her so timid and so dishonest in not being prepared to fulfil her part of the bargain.

'He has given me so much,' Dominica told herself miserably 'and now I am failing him when he relied on me.'

The idea brought the tears once again to her eyes and she realised that she felt tired and limp after her experience of the night before.

'I must get up,' she told herself.

But she lay watching the sunshine creeping into the room through the sides of the curtains and illuminating the decorations, which depicted the red lotus.

The bed had been carved in the same style as the one in her room, with petals painted the deep rose-red of the King of flowers. The curtains had a symbolic motif of lotuses, but the picture on the wall was different.

This was not of the Buddha. It was a beautifully painted picture of the lake in Kandy with the red lotus growing on it.

In the distance on the other side of the lake there was a glimpse of the Temple of the Sacred Tooth and hanging over the water were the Temple flower-trees in bloom as Dominica had seen them when she had driven there with Lord Hawkston.

It seemed to her in retrospect that it had been a day of inescapable magic.

She had never known such beauty existed and she could still feel the intensity of it.

Then, as she lay there gazing at the picture and remembering the scene, she suddenly understood why Kandy had seemed so beautiful, why the lake had shone with a strange mystical brilliance and why the beauty and colour of the flowers had seemed more vivid than she had ever known them.

It was because she had been with Lord Hawkston, because he was beside her, because she was acutely conscious of him and she was happy, happier than she had ever been in her whole life.

And the reason for her happiness came to her in a blinding light.

It was all so simple and yet she had not understood until now that what she felt had been *love*.

Love for Lord Hawkston!

The man who had brought her up into the hills to marry his nephew!

CHAPTER SEVEN

It was nearly noon before Dominica arose.

But when she was dressed and went from her room it was to find that the house was empty, neither Lord Hawkston nor Gerald were anywhere to be seen.

She picked up her sunshade thinking that she would go into the garden.

The new way that she had arranged her hair in in a corolla on top of her head was, she thought, becoming so that she decided she would not spoil it by wearing a bonnet.

Anyway there was no one to see her.

She had, however, just reached the front door when she heard the sound of a horse's hoofs and saw Lord Hawkston come riding down the path that led up the mountain.

He dismounted and she thought that his horse looked as if he had ridden it hard.

She also noticed that he wore a pistol in the belt that encircled his waist.

She supposed he had been out looking for the leopards, but it was difficult to think of anything except that her heart leapt at his appearance. At the same time she felt overwhelmingly shy.

His white shirt was open at the neck as it had been when she had seen him riding the previous morning and his sleeves were rolled up above his sunburnt arms.

"Where are you going?" he asked her with a smile.

She thought that his eyes rested appreciatively on the colourful muslin gown she wore with its full skirts and ribbons at the neck.

"I was just – going for a walk in the – garden before – luncheon," she replied wondering why it was hard to speak and the words seemed somehow constricted in her throat.

A servant led Lord Hawkston's horse away and he said,

"We have time, if it will please you, to look at the giant lotus."

"I would – like it – very much," Dominica replied breathlessly.

He turned to walk beside her across the lawn and she thought, as she had done before, how young and athletic he looked when he was dressed unconventionally.

Equally, because she loved him and was receptive to his moods, she had the feeling that he was worried about something and she hoped that he would tell her what it was.

But instead he talked about the garden, showing her the different flowers he had planted and pointing out the rare trees and shrubs, some of which Dominica had never even heard of before.

"In two months' time," he related, "the rhododendrons will be in flower. They blossom later in these high altitudes, but their colours are indescribable."

Dominica longed to ask him if he thought that she would be there in two months' time and then, even as the words trembled on her lips, she knew that she could not say them.

He trusted her, he believed in her and she remembered how, when they were in Kandy, she had told him that if one was really in love there was no sacrifice one would not make.

Well, she was in love and the sacrifice required of her was that she should do what Lord Hawkston wished and marry his nephew.

Even to think of it made her want to cry as she had cried last night on his shoulder, but she knew that to do so would make him despise her even more than he must do already.

He was being courteous and charming, because he wished to make it easy to forget the way she had run to him for protection and lain in his arms to cry against his shoulder.

At the time it had seemed the only thing she could do, but now that she was with him again, Dominica could not help blushing at the thought of how she had behaved.

It was true that at that moment she had not thought of him as a man but rather as a tower of strength, a comfort and a protector. But he was a man and she had known it when she had awoken in his bed to look at the picture on the wall in his room.

'I love him! I love him!' she told herself.

But she knew that she must never let him know of her feelings for him. Instead she must sacrifice her whole life to doing what he wished.

She tried to concentrate on what Lord Hawkston was saying and yet she could only think how thrilling it was to be beside him and how if he touched her arm accidentally or drew close to her as they inspected a flower or a bush, it sent a little tremor of excitement all through her body.

She wondered why she had not realised last night when she had wept against him and felt his arms holding her so securely that this was what she had wanted more than anything in the whole world.

She wondered now what he would think if she asked him to hold her once again and to give her that sense of security and protection which had finally swept away her fears so that she had fallen asleep still holding his hand.

'Could any man,' she asked herself, 'have been kinder or more understanding than him?'

She knew how angry her father would have been at her behaviour and she knew that everyone, if they learnt of it, would be shocked at the thought of her clinging to Lord Hawkston, wearing nothing but the thin lace-trimmed nightgown that was a part of her trousseau.

Had he thought her fast and brazen because of her behaviour?

She was certain that he thought of her merely as a rather tiresome child, a foolish girl who was afraid of the dark and who, though having lived all her life in Ceylon, was yet scared of two leopards fighting each other and being of no danger to her personally.

'I may seem a child to him,' Dominica told herself, 'but I love him as a woman. I love him with my whole being and I know that this is love as it is meant to be, love that has existed since the beginning of time.'

She knew that what she felt for Lord Hawkston was a spiritual yearning that was in fact part of the Divine.

It was something, she told herself, that Gerald would never understand.

How could she stay with a man year after year who was coarse and materialistic and without any sensitivity whatsoever?

How could she endure his whole attitude to life and, worst of all, how could she contemplate the moment when he would not only kiss her but they would be united as man and wife?

Instinctively, because she was once more afraid, she moved a little closer to Lord Hawkston.

As if he realised that something perturbed her, he said,

"Perhaps we are lingering too long. Come, I promised to show you the giant lotus before we return to the house for luncheon."

He led her from the garden down a path that had obviously been cut through the jungle.

On either side there were trees in bloom, but Dominica realised that the original path had narrowed because it had been left unattended and the undergrowth on either side of it had encroached so that in some places they had to walk singly.

But it was all very beautiful and the scent of the magnolias, the jasmines and the champees made her feel as if she was really in the Garden of Eden.

Then, almost unexpectedly, they came upon the pool they were seeking.

It was surrounded by trees that werew not very large. It was shaded from the sun that filtered through the branches, throwing a variegated pattern of gold and giving the clearing a strange mysticism that was difficult to describe.

The pool itself was breathtaking. Covered by the giant lotus, some of which were open and some in bud, it was a picture of colour and beauty that made Dominica draw in her breath because it was so lovely.

On the other side of the pool stood a pedestal where stood a statue of Buddha.

Lord Hawkston, following the direction of her eyes, then said,

"Here is one of my special treasures that I particularly wanted to show you. I think it originally came from

Anuradhapura, but I found it neglected and forgotten amongst some ruins in the jungle and I brought it here so that at least it has a reverent and appropriate setting."

"It has indeed," Dominica said, speaking for the first time since she had seen the pool.

"Come and look at the carvings on it," Lord Hawkston suggested.

They encircled the pool, having a little difficulty in pushing through the ferns and plants that had forced their way between the trees when there had been no gardeners to keep them under control.

They reached the statue of Buddha and Dominica realised that Lord Hawkston had placed it against a background of Temple trees and champees that were to be found near every Buddhist *wihara* on the island.

Buddhism, she knew, was the religion of flowers and she thought that Lord Hawkston was one of the few Englishmen who would have treated the sacred emblem of a religion other than his own with such reverence.

She thought as they reached the statue, which on its pedestal stood a little above them, that he looked annoyed to find the fig-ivy that climbs all over rocks and buildings was curling itself round the ancient grey stone.

He put out his hand to start pulling it away from where it was encroaching on the stone lotus where the Buddha was seated.

"It must be very old – " Dominica began when something, she was not certain what it was, made a movement that attracted her attention.

She turned her head and screamed.

Just behind them, having come silently through the undergrowth, was a man!

His face was contorted into a mask of demoniacal hatred, his arm was raised and in his hand was a wooden-handled sharp-pointed *kris*.

Without thinking, just acting as her instinct told her to save the man she loved, Dominica threw herself against Lord Hawkston as he bent over the stone lotus.

He staggered and the knife, which would have struck him in the base of the neck, missed.

Instead the sharp-pointed blade passed through the thick corolla of plaited hair that Dominica wore on top of her head, and the force of it threw her backwards so that she was impaled against the trunk of a tree.

It all happened so quickly that Dominica's scream of fear had hardly died away before Lord Hawkston, regaining his balance, had drawn his pistol and shot the madman who menaced them.

Even as he fired, Lord Hawkston realised that it was Lakshman, whom he had been seeking all the morning.

Lakshman threw up his hands as the bullet hit him in the chest and he fell backwards into the pool, his body splashing through the giant lotus.

Lord Hawkston turned to Dominica and realised that, after the shock of what had happened, she had fainted and was held upright only by the *kris,* which pinioned her through her hair to the tree.

Hastily he put his arm around her and drew out the knife, feeling a sudden fear because it was covered in blood.

Then, as he threw it to the ground and examined Dominica's head, he saw with relief that it was not her blood that stained it.

She was still unconscious and he picked her up in his arms and carried her round the side of the pool.

Only as he reached the path which led back to the house did he look down at the water and realise that there was no sign of Lakshman,

The lotus blossoms had closed again over the spot where he had fallen through them.

Except for the bloodstained *kris* lying at the foot of the statue of Buddha, there was nothing to show that murder had been attempted in that quiet spot and that two people had been saved from being massacred by only a hair's breadth and a frightened scream.

Holding Dominica closely in his arms, Lord Hawkston walked quickly down the path that led back to the house.

Only when he reached the cultivated part of the garden did he find Gerald.

His body was lying face downwards on the grass, his white shirt stained crimson where Lakshman had struck him in the back as he was walking home for luncheon.

*

Dominica stirred.

Vaguely she remembered coming back to consciousness more than once, but what she thought or felt had been very hazy.

Someone had given her something to drink and she had fallen asleep, again the deep dreamless sleep of complete oblivion.

Now she felt different. It was almost as if she could feel herself coming alive, her brain began to work and she was no longer sleepy.

Slowly she opened her eyes and for a moment it was difficult to imagine where she could be.

It was a room that she had never seen before and the bed that she was lying in was very large. There were two posts at the end of it reaching right to the ceiling.

The sunshine was coming through the curtains, which were only half-closed and the windows were open onto the verandah.

Suddenly Dominica was aware that she was in the room that Lord Hawkston had spoken about, the 'Palm Room', that he had built for himself and which Gerald had closed up.

At the thought of Lord Hawkston a little tremor went through her.

Now she remembered!

Slowly she recalled the contorted face of Lakshman when he had tried to kill him.

She had known without being told who the madman was, known that he was Seetha's father desiring revenge for the way that his daughter had been treated. He must have wished to kill not only Gerald Warren, who was responsible for her death, but also any white man connected with him.

Before she had fainted with the horror of what had occurred, she had heard the report of Lord Hawkston's pistol and seen Lakshman fall into the pool.

It was then a merciful darkness had covered her so she had known nothing more.

'I wonder how long ago it happened.' Dominica asked herself.

She had the feeling that some time had elapsed and yet she could be sure of nothing.

Surprisingly, she told herself, she was no longer afraid.

Perhaps it was because she was in Lord Hawkston's room and, although she was alone, it was as if the sense of protection he gave her lingered there on the atmosphere.

She looked up and was spellbound by what she saw.

The posts that she had noticed at the end of the bed were carved like palm trees, the ceiling was arched and palm branches were painted on it.

Now she looked around the room and realised that every six feet or so there were carved trunks of palm trees rising from the floor to the ceiling and between them vividly and skilfully executed were murals of the jungle.

There were trees, ferns and convolvuli, vines and rattans. There was the weaving plant, known as the *kudumirris*, which weaves itself from tree to tree.

There were lianas, which wove fantastic patterns in the treetops, falling to the earth in marvellous festoons. And, of course, there were the flowers, orchids of every shape, size and colour, magnolias and camellias, rhododendrons and roses.

It was all so beautiful and unexpected that Dominica could only lie against her pillows looking around her with delight.

There were the birds that she had known all her life, the crested eagle, the hawk, the martin and the swift.

There were also halcyons or kingfishers, small, red-billed and resplendent, their bodies sapphire-blue the bluest blue it was possible to imagine.

She could also see the green bee-eaters and the paradise flycatchers with their rich chestnut plumage, orioles black-headed and golden, the blue-tailed pittas and green pigeons.

How could Lord Hawkston have thought of having a bedroom so exciting, she thought in awe and so incredibly lovely?

She remembered he had told her that it was unique and she knew that there could not be a room in the whole world that was so different from everyone else's.

She raised herself a little higher on the pillows so that she could go on looking at it.

Now she could see that little monkeys had been painted in the trees and in one corner of the room there was the *walura* or boar, which Dominica knew was happy, grubbing and greedy, unless he was cornered, when he could become extremely vicious.

There were also glimpses through the exquisite foliage of a bear, a sambhur and a leopard.

But what were much more beautiful were the butterflies of every size and colour and the lizards, which Dominica had tried to tame ever since she had been as small as Prudence.

It was all like watching a fairy story being projected before her and she lay for a long time looking at it with fascinated eyes until she found herself wondering how many of Lord Hawkston's friends, especially those in England, would think him capable of creating such an imaginative fantasy.

'It is because he loves the country so much,' Dominica told herself, 'that he wants to keep it around him even when he is asleep.'

And she knew that, just as Lord Hawkston loved Ceylon, Gerald hated it.

The thought of Gerald made even the sunshine seem dark for a moment.

Then the door opened and a woman came in.

Dominica had never seen her before and yet she knew that she must have been aware of her even while she had been unconscious.

She was a smiling pleasant-faced Englishwoman, wearing a badly fitting white blouse and skirt, and her mousy hair had escaped untidily from a bun pinned at the back of her head.

"You are awake!" she said with a smile. "I thought you would be."

"How long have I been asleep?" Dominica enquired.

"For three days!" the woman replied and, as Dominica looked incredulous, she added,

"I had better introduce myself. I am Mrs. Smithson and I have been looking after you."

"Thank you," Dominica replied. "Are you a nurse?"

The woman crossed the room to draw back the curtains a little further and let in more sunshine.

"I am what they call a Medical Missionary," she replied. "But nurse is a better word, for if anyone is ill in this district I am the only person they can ask for unless they are prepared to travel all the way to Kandy."

She turned from the window towards the bed.

"I am glad you are awake, Miss Radford," she said, "because, as a matter of fact, I have come to tell you that I must leave."

"Have – have you told – Lord Hawkston?" Dominica stammered, a little bewildered.

"Lord Hawkston will be returning on the afternoon train from Kandy," Mrs. Smithson said. "He has been at the funeral."

"The funeral?"

"Of his nephew, Mr. Warren," Mrs. Smithson said quietly.

She saw Dominica stiffen and the surprise in her eyes.

"Lakshman killed him before he attempted to take Lord Hawkston's life," she explained. "His Lordship told me that you saved him!"

"Lakshman killed – Gerald?" Dominica repeated almost beneath her breath.

"He died instantly. A native *kris* is a very lethal weapon!"

Dominica said nothing and after a moment Mrs. Smithson went on,

"I am sorry about this. Everything that happened must have been a terrible shock for you. But I know you will realise that there is nothing you can do about it, except forget it. Such tragedies occur, but not often, I am glad to say."

"And – Lord Hawkston shot – Lakshman?" Dominica asked hesitatingly.

"He was quite mad, poor man," Mrs. Smithson replied. "As a matter of fact, when I treated him for an affliction in one of his eyes a few months ago, I thought that he was decidedly unhinged. He was a difficult man and no one would employ him."

She leant against the carved post of the bed and looked at Dominica.

"Forget it all, child and if you take my advice you will get up, go downstairs and be ready to greet Lord Hawkston when he arrives."

"How did you keep me asleep for so long?" Dominica enquired.

"It was his Lordship's idea," Mrs. Smithson said, "and, as it happens, I agreed with him. It was not anything drastic, just a few herbs that I give to women who are in pain to make them feel a bit 'muzzy'. You will be quite all right when you have had a cup of tea."

She gave a little laugh.

"I always say there is nothing like a good strong cup of our own tea to sweep away the cobwebs!"

She glanced at the clock.

"I will tell the servants to bring you up some and prepare your bath. I am sorry I cannot stay so that we can get to know each other, but doubtless we will meet again."

"Why are you leaving?" Dominica asked.

"That is what I came to explain," Mrs. Smithson replied. "Will you tell his Lordship that Mrs. Davison, whose husband is a planter on the other side of the hill, has started her first baby and they have sent for me? I know he will understand."

"I am sure he will," Dominica said, "and thank you very much for looking after me."

"It's been a pleasure," Mrs. Smithson smiled. "And, between ourselves, I would do anything for Chilton Hawk, I beg his pardon, Lord Hawkston. And please you tell him from me the longer he stays the better. We need him here."

"I will give him your message," Dominica said.

Mrs. Smithson held out her hand.

"Goodbye, Miss Radford. And try not to worry about what has happened. There is always tomorrow. That is what I always say!"

"I will try to do as you suggest," Dominica smiled.

Mrs. Smithson shook her hand heartily.

"Goodbye," she said again. "Take care of yourself. I will be popping in to see you one of these days."

When she had gone, Dominica lay back against the pillows.

So Gerald was dead!

It might be wrong it, might indeed be wicked, but she could not help feeling a sense of unutterable relief.

Now she would not have to marry him! Now she would be free of the promise she had given Lord Hawkston.

Then suddenly another problem presented itself.

Would this mean that she must go home immediately? That she could no longer stay here in the hills? That she must return to the life she had lived before Lord Hawkston had taken her into a world she had never known?

It was a world that contained drama and danger and strange passions, at the same time a world so beautiful and so wonderful that she knew it had changed her whole being.

Then with a sudden urgency that revived her like a glass of wine she knew that she wanted to see Lord Hawkston again, she wanted to talk to him, to be with him and for the moment she could think of nothing else.

*

Dominica was downstairs waiting in the sitting room when she heard the carriage that had met Lord Hawkston at the Station driving up to the front door.

The big doors of the house were always left open so that the cool air could blow through and now she was suddenly tense as she heard the servants greeting their Master and heard Lord Hawkston reply,

"I want to wash and put on something comfortable."

"Your bath is ready, *Durai*."

Dominica heard Lord Hawkston go upstairs. She knew that while he had given up his room to her he had slept in another that was on the same floor.

Already she had discovered that even in the three days she had been ill things had changed about the house.

There were many more servants and the place seemed to shine with a new cleanliness and brightness as she came down the stairs.

She had looked out into the garden and seen no fewer than five men working to cut back the encroaching jungle, replace the flowers that had been rooted up by the leopards and water the green lawns.

She thought too that some pieces of furniture had been moved and she guessed that they had been put back in the places that Lord Hawkston had originally planned for them.

The sitting room was filled with flowers and there had been big bowls of flowers in her bedroom. They had seemed almost a part of the murals on the walls.

But in the sitting room they now stood on every chest and table and in the hall there were great vases of lilies, which scented the whole house with their sweet fragrance.

Dominica had spent much longer than usual after she had had her bath in making herself look as attractive as possible.

She seemed thinner since her long sleep and her eyes seemed to fill the whole of her small heart-shaped face.

She could not bear to plait her hair and dress it as it had been before. Even to think of the corolla on her head was to remember the impact of Lakshman's *kris* as it had passed through it and pinioned her to the tree.

Instead she coiled it into a chignon at the back of her head and hoped that Lord Hawkston would not think it looked too old-fashioned.

She chose her prettiest gown and then when she had put it on, wondered if she should change into another.

She had the feeling that it was important to look her best because, although she would hardly face the fact, she knew that her whole future depended on what he was about to decide for her.

As she sat waiting in the sitting room, forcing herself to sit still with her heart thumping tumultuously in her breast, she knew that her lips were dry with fear.

While she longed irrepressibly to see him again, she was afraid that, when she did so, he would tell her that he expected her to go home at once perhaps tomorrow.

'How can I bear it? How can I face it?' Dominica asked herself.

She thought how humiliating it would be if she burst into tears and cried against him as she had done when she had been so frightened by the leopards.

Yet when he came into the room she felt her heart leap and it was impossible to speak, impossible to do anything but rise to her feet to stand looking at him, conscious that her knees were trembling.

"Dominica!" Lord Hawkston exclaimed, and she thought that he looked happy. "I was hoping you would be well enough to get up. But where is Mrs. Smithson? The servants tell me that she has gone away."

With a tremendous effort as if her voice came from very far away, Dominica replied,

"She asked me to – tell you she had to go to – Mrs. Davison who is having – a baby. She knew you would – understand."

Lord Hawkston walked nearer.

"I do understand," he said. "At the same time it is inconvenient."

Dominica felt her spirits drop.

He obviously did not want to be alone with her. He wanted Mrs. Smithson to be there, perhaps because it would prevent them from talking intimately.

The servants came in with cool drinks and some sandwiches. Lord Hawkston took a glass in his hand and walked towards the window.

"It was very hot in Kandy," he said in a conversational tone. "I was looking forward to being back."

The servants left the room but Dominica could find nothing to say. She could only stand gazing at him, thinking how handsome he was and how at ease he appeared in his white suit, and yet how elegant!

He turned and looked at her.

"How do you feel?"

There was a note of anxiety in his voice that had not been there before.

"I-I am – all right," Dominica answered.

"That is what I hoped you would say."

He put down his glass.

"It is, however, annoying," he went on, "that Mrs. Smithson has had to leave so quickly. I had hoped that she would be able to stay while we talked about your future and now you have no chaperone!"

"Is it so – important for me to have – one?" Dominica asked him.

"It is conventionally correct, as you well know."

He stood with his back to the fireplace and after a moment Dominica asked in a very small voice,

"Are you – sending me– away?"

He did not look at her, but stared towards the window as he replied,

"I have been thinking about that, Dominica, in fact I have thought of little else these past few days. It seems to me that there are two alternatives."

"What are – they?"

"The first, of course, is that you might return to your family," Lord Hawkston said. "And considering that you were so nearly married to my nephew, I think it only fair that I should settle a certain amount of money on you."

"That is – unnecessary!" Dominica said quickly.

"On the contrary I think it very necessary. At the same time I have a feeling that you might see very little of it and that your father would spend it on those he thought more needy than you."

This was so true that Dominica felt it did not need an answer.

"On the other hand," Lord Hawkston went on, "I can take you with me to England."

He looked at her as he spoke and saw the sudden gladness in her face that was like a light.

"Once we are there," he went on. "I can quite easily find you a suitable husband."

The light faded.

Dominica's eyes met his and it seemed as if neither of them could look away.

It was impossible to move, impossible to breathe.

Then she said in a voice that he could hardly hear,

"Let me – stay with – you."

"Do you know what you are asking? I am too old for you, Dominica."

Just for a moment it seemed as if she did not understand. Then she moved towards him swiftly and instinctively, seeking him as she had done the night that she had been so frightened.

His arms went round her and it was like reaching Heaven to feel them holding her as she wanted to be held.

"I said I am too old," he said in a strange voice that she had never heard from him before.

"I – love – you!"

She whispered the words and yet they were quite clear,

"Are you sure? Oh, my darling, are you sure?"

She lifted her face to his.

For a moment he looked down into her eyes and then he pulled her against him and his lips were on hers.

It seemed to Dominica as if the whole world was illuminated with a golden radiance that was blinding.

She felt that his lips possessed her and yet gave her everything that had ever been beautiful and moving, exquisite and lovely.

It was what she had sought in the music she had played or listened to on the breeze of the wind.

It was also what she had found in the brilliance of the flowers in Kandy and in the enchantment of the jungle.

"I love – you! *I love you!*"

She was not certain if she said it aloud or with the feelings he evoked in her, which seemed to pass from her lips to his.

She loved him so intensely that she felt already that she was a part of him, they belonged to each other, they were indivisible and no longer two people but one.

Finally Lord Hawkston raised his head.

"My precious, my darling," he exclaimed unsteadily. "This is wrong! You should find someone of your own age."

"There is only – you in the – whole world."

"Do you really mean that?"

"I think I knew it from the very first – moment I met – you," she whispered. "But I was not – aware that it was – love."

He kissed her again and she felt herself thrill and come alive with sensations such as she had never known existed.

Looking down at her face radiant with happiness he asked masterfully,

"When did you first know you loved me? Tell me I want to hear."

"I think I – loved you first when you were so – kind in giving each of the girls a new gown and bonnet and – when you told Madame Fernando that they were all to be different. I thought you were more understanding than – I could have expected any man to be."

She gave a little sigh of sheer happiness and continued,

"And when you were so clever with Prudence – telling her she must eat her food so that she could go to her ball – you would give for her, I knew – "

Dominica's voice faltered for a moment and a blush arose in her cheeks.

"What did you know, my sweet?"

"I – knew that was how I would like the – father of my children to – behave with them," she murmured and hid her face against his neck.

He held her so tightly that it was impossible to breathe.

"And when did you first admit to yourself that you loved me?"

"When we were at Kandy," she answered. "It was so beautiful that I could think of nothing but – love. Then afterwards, when I saw the picture in your bedroom I knew why. It was because I – loved you. I loved you with all of me – but I thought you would – despise me."

"I loved you from the very first moment," Lord Hawkston said. "I realised what a hard life you were living and I wanted to take you out of it to protect you!"

He paused before he went on,

"I have never before in my whole life wanted to protect and take care of a woman, not for my own pleasure but for hers. I wanted to shelter you from harm, to stand between you and anything that could hurt or distress you."

"That is why I – ran to you when I was – frightened," Dominica told him. "I knew I would be safe – with you."

"As you always will be," Lord Hawkston said. "And when I saw you in your Wedding gown, I knew that you were the embodiment of everything a man could desire and long for in a bride. You were beautiful, exquisitely beautiful and yet at the same time I had already learnt how much character and personality you had."

He kissed her forehead.

"Will you wear that gown tomorrow for me, my darling, when we go to Kandy to be married?"

She turned her face up to his and her eyes seemed full of stars.

Then he felt her stiffen and she dropped her head.

"What is it?" he asked.

"I had forgotten," she said in a low voice, "that in England you are very – important. I have been thinking about you only as living here – a planter. Perhaps you will be – ashamed of me amongst your smart friends."

Lord Hawkston put his hand under her chin and turned her face up to his again.

"I have no friends who you would not shine more brilliantly amongst than the sun itself." he said. "You are mine, Dominica, *mine*, as you were always meant to be and perhaps you have been in the past Now that you have said that you love me, I will never let you go."

"That is all I want," Dominica cried, "to be – yours for all Eternity."

"That is what you will be," he said, "and because I think it will please you and because too I want it myself, I intend that we shall live here for six months of each year. It does not take long to travel to England. We will go back in the summer and do our duty for the family and the estate, but for the winter we will return here. Will that make you happy?"

"You know it – will!" Dominica answered, "And you know too that I will be happy anywhere – anywhere in the world – as long as I can be with you."

There was a note in her voice that brought the fire into Lord Hawkston's eyes.

Then his lips were on hers and he was kissing her until she could no longer think, but only feel that her heart and soul were both his.

*

The stars were very brilliant in the sky as Dominica and Lord Hawkston came from the Palm Room onto the verandah.

Dominica was wearing the white gown that she had been married in earlier in the day.

She had changed for the train journey, but, when she had come home, she had put on her Wedding gown again because she knew that Lord Hawkston liked to look at her in it.

It had been a very simple and quiet Wedding with only James Taylor as their Best Man, but to Dominica it had been a Service of dedication and she had known that Lord Hawkston felt the same.

She had heard James Taylor say when the Service was over,

"I am happy for you, Chilton, you always needed a wife."

"To keep me in order?" Lord Hawkston answered with a smile.

"To complete the story of your success!" James Taylor had replied. "When you have finished honeymooning, come and see me. I have not only new methods of tea dyeing to show you but I have also a young man who is just the sort of Manager you need. He has been out here for two years and you can trust him."

"Thank you, James," Lord Hawkston smiled.

It had been very moving for Dominica to arrive back at the house and know that it was to be her home with the man she loved.

As she saw it standing over the valley like a precious jewel encircled by the gardens and the silver lake, her fingers had tightened on her husband's hand.

"We will be happy!" she declared.

"I know now that I built it for you," he answered, "and there was always something missing when I was in the Palm Room."

Dominica blushed and he kissed her hand.

"You need never be afraid of being alone in the darkness again, my lovely one."

They had so much to say to each other and so much to talk about that they had lingered long over the superlative dinner that the cook had provided for them.

Now as they stepped onto the verandah it was too late to see the sunset.

Dominica looked up.

There was a half-crescent moon moving up the sky and, as Lord Hawkston followed her eyes, he said quietly,

"Do you know what the crescent moon is called by our people?"

"No – tell me."

She knew that even the sound of his voice made little tremors of excitement run through her and the fact that his arm was around her made her quiver and long for the touch of his lips.

"It is called a 'lovers' moon'," Lord Hawkston said, "and that, my precious wonderful wife, is what it means to us."

"A lovers' moon – over the Garden of Eden!" Dominica said softly. "What lovers could ask for more?"

"What indeed?" he agreed, "and no man could ask for more than to have you as his wife!"

She raised her face to his and in the light from the sky he could see her expression of happiness very clearly.

"You are *so* beautiful," he said, "so exquisitely perfect. I want to tell you something."

"What is it?" Dominica asked.

"When I first came to Ceylon," he said, "and I was only twenty-one, I thought, as I suppose all young men do, that sooner or later I would find someone I would love and we would get married. But what happened was very different."

Dominica looked at him a little apprehensively as he went on,

"I fell in love not with a woman, my darling, but with a country. I loved Ceylon! It seemed to me everything that a man could wish to find in the woman he would love. It was soft and warm, sweet and friendly, and besides giving a man so much materially it also had a spiritual message for those who would listen to it."

"I can understand that," Dominica whispered.

Lord Hawkston kissed her hair and it smelt of the fragrance of the jasmine buds she had entwined amongst the orange blossom wreath that Madame Fernando had made for her.

It was the fragrance of Ceylon, he thought, a fragrance that was irresistible and wholly feminine.

"Sometimes," he went on, "when I stood on this verandah, I used to think that I would be alone for the rest of my life. No one, I thought, could ever mean to me what this country had come to mean. No woman could ever be so beautiful or so utterly and completely desirable."

His arms tightened around her.

"Then I found you! And I knew that you were all that I wanted, all that I had dreamt of and all that I had thought of as the utter and complete perfection that any woman could attain."

"Suppose I – fail you?" Dominica asked in a breathless little voice.

"You could never do that!" he answered. "We shall doubtless have our difficulties, setbacks, perhaps even storms, like the rains that fall on the valley, but fundamentally we are one, we belong to each other, Dominica, and nothing can change or alter that."

"Another Adam and Eve!"

She felt his lips against the softness of her skin.

"You are my Eve," he said. "I love you with all the love that exists in the whole world and I will spend my life making you sure of it."

He drew her closer as he spoke and now their lips met and Dominica put her arms round his neck to draw him closer still.

"I love – you! *I love – you!*"

She felt his hands on her hair drawing the pins from it so that it fell in a silken wave over her shoulders.

He kissed it, then sweeping it aside he kissed her neck, her shoulders, and as he unfastened her gown and it slipped lower, her rose-tipped breasts.

"You are like a lotus flower," he said passionately. "I worship you."

Then he drew her gently, his lips holding her captive, back into the Palm Room and the curtains closed behind them.

Outside the lovers' moon rose slowly up the starlit sky throwing its mystical silver light over the sleeping valley

OTHER BOOKS IN THIS SERIES

The Barbara Cartland Eternal Collection is the unique opportunity to collect all five hundred of the timeless beautiful romantic novels written by the world's most celebrated and enduring romantic author.

Named the Eternal Collection because Barbara's inspiring stories of pure love, just the same as love itself, the books will be published on the internet at the rate of four titles per month until all five hundred are available.

The Eternal Collection, classic pure romance available worldwide for all time.